the IMPOSSIBLE SPY

by Kirby Carr

MAJOR BOOKS • CHATSWORTH, CALIFORNIA

THE FEDERAL BUILDING was a black granite dark-windowed glittering high-rise jutting toward the Los Angeles sky, containing on its upper floors the memory banks and brain data of the Strategic Arms Division, U.S. Air Force. The lobby was large and spacious, with glass entrance doors at the front and revolving doors at the side directly off the big parking lot on Veteran Avenue.

There were two security guards in the lobby, Bannon and Keller. Tough beefy men, they were stationed behind the high counter toward the rear of the lobby near the elevators. There was a chattering gizmo behind the counter ledge which they put on closed packages and attaché cases, and a red sign with white lettering reading:

PLEASE CHECK BELONGINGS HERE AND BE AUTHORIZED TO CONTINUE. NO ONE ADMITTED WITHOUT CLEARANCE.

Surface street noises filtered through the lobby doors, and the banks of elevators hummed softly at the rear. The early morning work force had already gone through, and the first wave of visitors; so Bannon and Keller relaxed, smoking.

At precisely 10:08 on this Friday morning in July, the revolving side doors spun and a man came through. He was tall and slender, the only other person in the lobby, and his heels made sharp echoing sounds as he strode directly ahead toward the elevators.

Keller tapped the gun holstered on his right hip and nudged Bannon. Bannon looked up, frowned, and put up his hand. The visitor had come up even with the counter ledge and was about to go past. A thin black attaché case dangled from his arm.

"Hold it," Bannon said. "Right there."

Keller grinned and tapped the counter in front of him. "Over here, please. You have to be checked in."

The man stopped, looked at the elevator wall fifty steps ahead, turned and stepped toward the guards.

"I'll take it, Harry," Bannon said, and Keller nodded and picked up the formsheet he had been studying.

The man was closer now, dark-eyed, face expressionless, and Ed Bannon smiled at him to put him at ease. "I got to check what you're carrying, sir, before you go up. Please set it up on top here, and give me your name and the person you wish to see."

The man looked at him and Bannon noticed he

was very tan from the sun and had a soft mocking look in his bright eyes. The man did nothing but stand there, and Bannon thought there was something he was supposed to do but couldn't think what it was. The geiger gizmo next to him started its chatter and Bannon liked the sound and nodded, feeling very relaxed and at peace with the world.

The man stepped back smiling and Bannon nodded thinking of a time many years ago when he was a kid and going bare-ass in old Muller's creek. The man was walking steadily toward the rear elevators now, walking smoothly, his heels sending up a sharp clattering sound, and Bannon remembered how it was the first time he grabbed for Susie Carter's tits and found them hard as apples.

At 10:15 the guard Keller yawned, threw down his formsheet and stretched. "Jesus, what a slow day!"

Bannon nodded. "Yeah. It sure was nice."

Keller lit another butt. "I guess that tall guy was the only one we had in nearly an hour."

"What tall guy?" Bannon said.

"The one you were just talking to. You were checking him out, Ed."

"I was?" Bannon blinked and looked down at the registration ledger. His finger went up and down. "I got nothing down here since 9:17. . . ."

"Come on," Keller said. "You was talking to him a minute ago. I heard you checking him out on the gizmo."

Bannon shrugged and rubbed his nose. "What time was he here?"

Keller stared. "Jesus, don't you remember?"

Bannon shook his head slowly and then both guards craned to look back at the elevators. Keller slipped out from behind and began running. Bannon picked up the telephone.

"Security here, Bannon speaking," Bannon barked into the phone. "Gimme Parson, third floor—" He didn't like the dead sound he had and began banging the cradle release. Nothing happened. "Hello, hello, goddammit," Bannon raged. "Wake up, ya dumb broad—"

He looked up and saw Keller walking back shaking his head. "Anything?" Bannon said, putting the phone down.

Keller frowned. "I dunno."

"I mean," Bannon said, "did you check with Parson upstairs?"

Keller shook his head. "Couldn't get up. Damn elevator won't move. Seems like a power short. How'd you do on the phone?"

Bannon sniffed, his beefy face turning dark red. "Nothing. The goddam phone's dead." He picked it up again, listened, set it down.

Keller and Bannon stared at each other. Bannon glanced at his watch. "We'll catch hell for this. I gotta report the damn phone went dead. My watch says 10:08—what you got?"

Keller looked at his and nodded. "The same, Ed. 10:08."

"You better check the stairs, Harry," Bannon said.

Keller turned. "Okay. What the hell did that guy look like anyway?"

Bannon thought about it. He rubbed his face. "Jesus, I don't remember."

The elevator doors swished open at the fifteenth floor and Gelson stepped out. The doors started to close behind him. Gelson stopped and looked at the closing doors and willed them to stay open.

8

A thin vein throbbed on his left temple, and he put out his hands. When his hands were extended about three feet away from the closing doors, they suddenly flew back and remained open.

Gelson walked to the elevator opposite, leaned forward and concentrated. He heard a humming noise and then it died down. He walked to the other elevators on the floor, and did the same at all six of them. When he heard nothing but silence, and then his own heartbeat, he nodded and turned away. "You're a killer, Guri," he said to himself. "Try to remember how you did that."

He stroked his left temple with thin sensitive fingers until the throbbing ebbed, and walked along the narrow hallway. There was nothing he could do now about the sudden appearance of any of the personnel working behind the closed doors. Gelson breathed in slowly and hoped for the best.

At the far end of the hall was a door marked: *DO NOT ENTER. AUTHORIZED PERSONNEL ONLY. RECORDINGS.*

Gelson tried the door and found it locked. He looked down at the double locks and sighed. They looked new and formidable.

He concentrated on the locks, forcing his mind to focus on the metal tumblers inside. *Open, you BASTARDS!* he commanded silently. *This is Guri Gelson speaking, your master.*

His temples throbbed madly, and he alternated his concentration from right to left temple. Unconsciously, he held his breath now trying to focus the force of his energy. The cords in his neck raised to thick pulsing ropes. "Come on, you bastards—give in!" he said under his breath, and heard the snapping sound immediately inside the doorframe. He inclined his head maintaining

9

the pressure he had built up.

He tried the door again and this time it opened. Gelson shook his head admiringly. "Thanks a lot. You're really good. You know that?"

Gelson closed the door quietly behind him. The room was a large windowless rectangle. Banks of computers on the far wall, files running along the left side. There were six tall rows of metal files running the width of the room, and Gelson walked up and down the narrow dark aisles until he found what he was looking for.

The file was marked: *SECRET. TESTING. PACIFIC ISLANDS (EAST). Warning: DO NOT REMOVE. DO NOT EXPOSE TO LIGHT.*

Gelson put his hand on the file drawer and saw the lock. *Damn, you're gonna give me a headache!* He bent toward it, focussing again, feeling the sweat now trickling down his face. He tested the drawer again. Nothing was happening. Come on, give, you sonofabitch, he raged inwardly. Was he giving it too much, too little? More left temple? More right? Gelson was never sure.

Focus, he told himself. Forget the logistics. *Focus!* He strained his entire being, his guts, staring down at it for ten seconds. Nothing happened and Gelson swore and turned away impatiently. He took a breath, swung his arms, rubbed his hair. There were always going to be days like this, he knew, as there had been before. This infuriating erratic talent of his that came and went like the breeze. One day you had it and could do miracles; and the next, nothing and you were a bum and—

He heard the snapping sound as the lock disengaged.

Gelson shook his head almost embarrassed. He didn't like it when things happened after he had concentrated. It was too hairy. But he sighed gratefully. As he stepped back to the stubborn file drawer, he heard the files all around him, clicking and snapping, doors shooting open, the whole damn wall of them shimmering and shaking as if some robot, some incredible electronic locksmith had swooped down from another planet with all the keys to the universe and its secrets.

"All right," Gelson said under his breath. "Enough already. You'll wake up the army." He pulled the file drawer out and saw the rows of tapes, wheel after wheel packed closely, head to head, filling the long dark recesses of the steel drawer.

"Okay, you mothers, this is Guri Gelson. I'm giving you five seconds, and that's it. Come on now, give!" He glowered down at the tapes, sweat streaming down his face. And then he saw the spools jump, the tapes spring out and curl and writhe like snakes, like flowers waving their tendrils.

Gelson held his hands over the writhing thin curling strips, and they collapsed as if they had been shot down. All the images would be erased now, he knew. He didn't know how, but that wasn't his problem. It was the world's. It worked, it was part of the crazy things he could do mentally, or chemically, or wishfully—Gelson shook his head. "Come on, Guri, don't beat it to death. When they want you to know, maybe they'll drop you a letter."

He didn't want to ruin the whole history of the world up here in the Federal Building where the Army of the United States locked up part of its war secrets. Just enough to do what he had to do.

Walking quickly away from the file, he found the one he needed to remove. It was marked:

N E U R O L O G I C A L : Short-Term—L o n g -
Term Memory.

No sooner had Gelson stepped up to it, than
the drawer slid open as if a genie had commanded
it. "Boy, you're hot now, kid. Don't lose it. Don't
lose it, don't abuse it."

He reached in and removed three spools and
put them inside his attaché case. He wondered if
he should take more, thought about it, shrugged,
and reached in for the rest. He stuffed those
that would not fit into the black case into his
pockets, under his shirt and belt. "Okay," he
told himself, "let's go." As he walked away, more
file drawers popped open. Gelson shook his head.
"It should only work so well on erections," he
said and went out.

When he was only a few steps from the near
elevator, one of the closed official doors opened.
Gelson held his breath. A young and pretty girl
walked out. She saw Gelson and smiled. "Nice
day," Gelson said.

"Maybe for you," the girl said. "I'm going
down for some coffee. My boss is giving me a
headache." She stepped inside the elevator, looking at Gelson. "You going down?" As he hesitated,
she said, "There's a cafeteria downstairs, just off
the main lobby."

Gelson nodded. He stepped inside. The girl
punched the button marked *L*. Nothing happened.
She punched it again and the door remained open.
The girl glanced at her watch and clucked irrit-
ably.

"Allow me," Gelson said. He passed his hand
over the buttons on the cable wall. "Abacadabra,
and all that. Let's go. The girl wants coffee."

The door swished close and the car began its
descent.

The girl smiled. "Thanks. I never would have thought of that."

Gelson shrugged. "I like to show off. By the way, what time is it, miss?"

She glanced at her wrist. "Ten-thirty-eight."

The elevator door opened at the lobby floor and she stepped out. She looked back and Gelson waved from the car. The door closed, the elevator hummed, and he disappeared from sight.

Keller nudged Bannon. "Look!" he said hoarsely.

They followed the elevator panel's red light and when the girl stepped out they were there on each side of her, guns out, two beefy men breathing hard.

"What the hell is this, Harry?" the girl said. "Since when you robbing the Air Force?"

Bannon stepped back sheepishly, mumbling apologies. His sidekick brushed him aside. "Miss Quimby, we're sorry. Did anybody come down with you? Did you see anybody on the way?"

"Sure. A man came down in the car with me."

"What floor did he get off?"

"He didn't. He kept going. I guess he wanted the basement."

Keller and Bannon exchanged frightened glances and jumped for the elevator. They pressed the *Up* button frantically. The girl stood there as the car came up and both men leaped in. The door stayed open as Bannon and then Keller jabbed at the button.

"Try saying abacadabra," the girl said. "That's what he did."

They were shaking their heads, jumping up and down, and swearing as she went across the lobby into the cafeteria.

...2

GELSON WAS TWENTY-FIVE years old, and had spent three of them before he fell out of his crib one night. He had the trick all set inside his head before he had finished yelling. At least, that was the story he told everybody interested in how he did the weird tricks. Maybe it was the fall and maybe it wasn't but somehow that kind of explanation made acceptable sense to his listeners. Nobody ever wanted to know a kid with strange powers, able to read your mind, stop your clock, melt your zipper, tell your future or make objects move unless it was an accidental freak thing.

Falling on your head could scramble your brains, as anybody knew, and you could go on from there and add the stuff that was mind blowing. What else can you expect if you lit on your head and broke some of the delicate stuff in there? Otherwise you had to be psychic, in league with the dead or worse yet, the Devil. Nobody wanted that.

Gelson had thought a lot about it, trying to pinpoint the thing exactly. Was it the bright light coming ever nearer from the sky one day that had searched him out and exploded in his brain, tagging him as one for Them? His mother had shaken her head firmly, said, "Don't believe that nonsense, you were lying in the sun too long. Anybody could get a headache from that."

Her grandmother could do strange things, she remembered, sensing at a great distance when something was wrong with one of the family. She had cried out one night that her favorite sister was dead. She could see the accident a thousand miles away, smell the fire, the molten metal of the overturned car. A telegram the following day from a survivor confirmed the dream.

Grandma was also good with cards, able to predict when something good or bad was about to happen. Eventually the cards came up consistently with dire warnings, and Grandma who didn't want to scare anybody, gave up her parlor trick.

Young Guri listened, shrugged, and admitted it could have been inherited; something like that, a minor genetic overdose of ESP molecules, coming to a kind of fruition in his own lifetime. Perhaps his kids, if he ever had any, would carry on. Move buildings, siphon money from banks.

The last thought was a constant nightmare with Guri, because as he grew up, trying to start with what he really knew for sure, there was the one constant. His family was poor. His father was French, an army officer, his mother Lebanese. When the war was over, his father found out he couldn't cut it in the civilian world, hampered by bad lungs and an unsteady heart. He loved to eat, was grossly overweight; and one day it all caught up to him and he died lifting one more forkful.

They had relatives in the United States, and Mrs. Gelson and her son arrived in upstate New York to stay with her sister and husband, their three sons, and five hundred cherry and apple trees. Guri tried to earn his keep picking the fruit, and subsequently fell from enough trees to unscramble whatever inside his head had originally been merely scrambled. But They didn't want it that way, apparently, and his uncanny psychic powers became stronger and more frequent.

By the time he finished his elementary schooling, he could pick a lock without touching it. Merely by staring at the locking mechanism in his strange way made the lock so nervous it gave up. Watches and clocks were easy. He merely stood near them and they stopped, or started again if they had been broken.

He was only eleven when the first spoon curled in his hand, and Guri stared down at it, looking at the curved handle, wondering how he had done that. He picked up five spoons in a row and each bent mysteriously. Guri put them down a little frightened. "Why?" he softly asked the Universe. "What's it all about, please? And why me?"

They didn't bother explaining.

He moved his first solid object mentally when he was fourteen. The girl across the seat from him in school had a brightly colored pencil he fancied, and as he sat there in class he wished he had one just like that. The pencil moved away from her hand and slid off the desk.

When the girl looked at him nervously, wondering if he had seen that, Guri nodded. He pointed to the open window. There wasn't the faintest sign of a breeze but he convinced her. "Wind current caught it. Rolled it right off."

When he was sixteen, his mother remarried and Guri was never comfortable with his stepfather. He began looking for work farther and farther away, and eventually wound up in New Jersey at a bowling ball factory, talking himself into the travelling job of sales rep.

The army got him a few years later, and he did his time at various state posts, specializing in Signal Corps work, learning to fool around with telephone repair, magnetic tapes, and broadcast equipment. It was during this period that he discovered to his dismay that any tape near his fingertips somehow became erased. If he wanted to think about it, concentrate on the spool itself, he could make it wind or unwind.

To protect himself and his secret, he learned to put his mind on something else when he was in the recording room, kept his hands in his pockets, and never came near a tape when an officer was around without inserting a pencil between his teeth. The lead somehow short-circuited his unbidden power, and Guri chewed through several hundred of them before he was given his Good Conduct medal and general release.

He decided to try his luck in California where he heard they had lots of bowling balls, and pretty girls in bikinis. Much to Guri's chagrin, he had no more power over girls than anybody else. He couldn't bend them to his power, move

17

them in any way; and the only time he had any luck at all was when some sweet young thing decided to have a try at the serious-looking young man who kept his hands in his pockets a lot, and sometimes a pencil in his mouth.

There wasn't anything special about his love-making, and sometimes his mind raced on ahead projecting other programs. There were the times when the pretty young things wondered if this tall and handsome fellow was really worth the trouble. And Guri would stammer his apologies and try to explain that he was a science-fiction writer—or trying to become one—and his book was taking shape in his mind and therefore the energy had gone to join his thoughts, as it will tend to do.

But his luck changed one day when he was sitting in a small and inexpensive restaurant, waiting for his date to show up, and amusing himself by staring the silverware on his table into pretzel-like shapes. A man came over from a table near the wall, said he had been observing him, introduced himself as a theatrical agent, and asked to see those tricks again.

Guri shrugged. He had never found a sensible use for his strange gifts, and he had a certainty that his date was out with somebody else and was going to stiff him. He was mad enough then to bend some more spoons, move an ashtray without touching it, and stop the stranger's timepiece.

"That's very interesting," the agent said. "I must have missed your act. What club do you work at?"

Gelson smiled. "I don't work at it. It's something I do that I try to forget."

"Not a bad idea," the man said, "unless you'd rather be making a thousand a week."

Guri lost his smile and asked what the man was talking about. The man handed him his card. On it, embossed in thin black letters, Guri read: *Sam Pine. Theatrical Agency. Talent for Night Clubs and TV.*

"I can book you by this weekend. A small club for openers. You break in your act. Get yourself comfortable with what you do. Then we make waves and get into the big time."

Guri scratched his head. The idea of making money this way had never crossed his mind. "But what would I do?"

The agent shrugged. "Whatever you just showed me. Bend spoons. Move ashtrays by looking at them. Stop watches."

"There's one thing," Guri said. "Maybe it's important."

"Like what?"

"It doesn't always work. Or again, sometimes I try and nothing happens no matter how I concentrate. But when I start to walk away, the trick happens."

The agent smiled. "Good for you. Seeing as how you and I are going places together, Gelson, why don't you level with me? What's your hidden gimmick? However you do it, it's terrific sleight of hand."

"There is no gimmick, hidden or otherwise. I do it mentally."

The agent bent forward, cupping one ear. "Say that again."

"Mentally. Like I can read minds, too."

Sam Pine sat back in his chair. "Okay, kid. Here's your chance. Tell me what I'm thinking."

Guri smiled. "Well, right now you're thinking 'Jesus, this is really a goldmine I got here and the kid is such a jerk I can probably take him for twice ten percent!' "

"Forget I mentioned it," the agent said. "Write down where I can reach you and we'll get going on this."

That was the start and as Sam Pine got him other clubs to work, Guri found he had finally discovered his bent. It was show business. Somehow the idea of appearing before a lot of strangers and amazing them with his tricks, hearing them applaud, seeing the surprise and incredulity on their faces, turned him on. He floated, and was inspired to giving even better performances.

Word got around about Gelson, the Psychic Wonder. *"He can move mountains with a thought!"* He made appearances with top TV celebrities—Johnny Carson, Merv, Steve—and one time he confounded an audience, estimated in the millions, by telling the viewers to bring their broken clocks out and he would heal them by mental vibrations. His boast came true and the network switchboard was jammed with thousands of callers screaming about their old clocks and watches, that hadn't worked in years, were now ticking away madly.

Sam Pine got better bookings for him and his pay went up to five thousand a week. Guri accepted it gladly, wondering how long the trick would last, feeling he might as well make it now while he had it, have some fun with his life before one day it was all gone.

But then some scientists who had observed his work made disturbing static. Guri Gelson, it seemed, was violating all the preconceived notions of science. Obviously, he was a fraud, a trickster, hoodwinking a gullible public.

Guri, outraged, offered himself as a guinea pig

willing to be tested openly by any group of scientists, under any conditions. The only stipulation he made was his usual one—that this thing was beyond his control and at times there would be a failure; he could guarantee nothing.

The University of California in Los Angeles at Westwood was the first to offer its facilities and psychic researchers to test Guri. Gelson wanted more. Not merely the psychic ones, he said. He wanted the best they had to look him over, to test what he could do. Perhaps one of them might understand what it was, this strange energy that defied natural laws. It might be useful to the world, provide another dimension in physics.

The scientists applauded and proceeded to put Gelson through their own kind of wringer. And when the tests were over, they were speechless, almost frightened by what he had done under stringent test conditions. Apparently, it was decided, Guri Gelson had a kind of energy not yet seen on this earth!

A visiting Soviet research gentleman sent word back to his superiors. A Chinese scientist cabled his country. An aide to the British Prime Minister dropped word to interested parties in her Majesty's government. France and Italy sent out couriers after reading the results of the test. Within two weeks, there were at least twenty interested keen-eyed representatives of various countries vying for a chance to speak to Mr. Gelson.

And a man named Adams, working in State, was wondering what would happen if a certain foreign government managed to somehow inveigle Guri Gelson into visiting their country.

"What would happen?" an aide asked.

Adams rolled his eyes. "Think about it. Gelson can disrupt radar equipment, eradicate magnetic tape, transport and dematerialize solid objects, stop machinery, influence geiger counters with a strong electromagnetic force no living human has." He rubbed his eyes wearily. "Can you imagine what would happen if he were trained, or let's say, forced to use his talents against us—against the civilized world?"

The aide shook his head, paling at the thought. "Okay, how do you want to work it?"

Adams said, "Give me the head of National Security, and send Boyle, the CIA man, up here right away. Maybe they have their ways about a delicate matter like this."

The department heads were of one mind, and that same night Guri was picked up by agents of the U.S. government and brought by army jet to Adams.

"We're not worried, of course, Mr. Gelson," Adams told him. "Actually those tests taken at the university don't prove very much. Have you been approached yet by any government to become a spy?"

"No," Guri said, gazing directly at Adams. "You're the first, Mr. Adams."

... 3

IT WOULD BE A TEST, Adams had said. The Federal
Building had tight security at the lower level,
and upstairs where the memory banks were and
the brain data. Everything was under lock and
key. There were, in addition, secretly placed cameras unobtrusively running twenty-four hours a
day, filming anybody entering the data research
room, following him closely every step of the
way.

"You get the items I mentioned," Adams had
said, "and I'll believe the reports on you. One
thing you'll have to remember—I can't guarantee
you any protection."

Guri thought about it. "Why the hell not?"

Already he had visions of being shot down before his career had really begun.

Adams shrugged. "It's just not done. There would be one hell of a stink, Mr. Gelson, if word got around that the State Department was aiding and abetting entry to its most secret files."

"Well," Guri said, "I like the way you do business. If you don't mind, I'd like to think about it."

"Fine," Adams said, rubbing his hands and catching the eye of Boyle, the CIA man.

"How about a piece of paper," Guri said. "You know, something that says I really didn't mean to do it."

"Hardly," Adams replied frostily. "I'd be laughed out of my job. And whether you realize it or not, Mr. Gelson, it is rather an important one."

"I dunno," Guri said. "It seems like I can get killed doing this. I'm no real spy, you know. Just an entertainer."

"So we've heard," Adams said. "But according to the reports we have been receiving, right at this moment there are at least ten foreign governments planning to get hold of you and your talents."

Guri looked surprised. "No kidding?"

Adams nodded. "Try to imagine for one moment, Mr. Gelson, your chances of refusal should any one of them bag you for their own purposes."

"Yeah," Guri said. "I see what you mean."

"On the other hand," Adams said, "should the government of the United States employ you in this rather extraordinary capacity, you may rest assured we would do everything to see that you are well protected."

"Well," Gelson replied, "like what would I be

doing working for you people?"

Adams sighed. "Pretty much the same thing, I'm afraid. We could call it a new form of psychic counter-espionage."

Gelson didn't like what he was hearing, but he thought perhaps maybe this was why They had given him the strange powers. To help his country. Certainly it didn't make sense otherwise, to go around folding spoons, stopping clocks, opening locks—there always had to be a larger design for this kind of screwy talent. At least, that was what he had always hoped.

This could be it, he told himself, what you were programmed for. What'll it hurt to try? If it don't work, so they'll can you and you can go back to working the clubs. "Okay," he told Adams. "When do I start?"

Adams looked at a slip of paper. "Tomorrow at precisely 10:08."

"Okay. What do I do with the stuff after I get it?"

"Don't worry about that," Adams said. "You'll be contacted as soon as you arrive home."

"I go straight back to my pad after cracking the Fed Building?" Guri asked.

Adams nodded. "Precisely."

"I don't go out at night?"

Adams shook his head. "Not until our men have seen you and relieved you of the, er, evidence."

"How will I know it's kosher? You know, that it will be the right guys?"

"You're supposed to be the mind reader," Adams had said stiffly.

"Oh, yeah. I forgot."

As he was leaving, Adams asked, "Do you know where the Federal Building is?"

25

Guri shook his head. "That's okay. Maybe I'll be able to think of it."

Adams blew his cheeks out and handed Guri a slip of paper with an address scribbled down. "Here's the information you will want. When you're finished memorizing it, destroy it."

Guri had looked down at the memo slip. "But it's only an address of a building. Is this a secret document?"

"Please, Mr. Gelson. We'd prefer it if you did things our way."

Guri handed the slip of paper back. "Okay. I got it. Here, you destroy it. I wouldn't want that kind of responsibility."

"You're being ridiculous," Adams said. "It's only the street address of a building."

"You keep it," Guri had said. "Right now, I got enough to worry about.

Gelson left the Federal Building a few minutes after the pretty girl in the elevator had given him the time. Ten-thirty-eight. The elevator car took him to the basement, and a flight of steps brought him to the outside of the building. He walked steadily toward his car in the parking lot beside the building without any alarm being sounded. He got his car door open, and was stepping inside, when he was struck over the head violently from behind, and fell unconscious before he could get a look at his assailants.

Adams wasn't happy when he got the news. "Sonofabitch," he said. "Now he's taken a walk to the other side with the stuff. Just goes to show you can't trust anybody."

Stanley the other CIA man lit a fresh cigar. "I think the big point you're missing here, sir, is

26

that Gelson did the impossible. Every item we requested from the files is gone. And in addition—"

Adams looked up. "What's this?"

Stanley went ahead doggedly. "He took a lotta stuff from the file on Neurological, short and long-term memory."

"What's it on?"

"It's the most comprehensive study made to date on all the psychic stuff. The same mental phenomena Gelson uses so effectively."

"I don't get it," Adams said plaintively. "Since he's so good at it, why the hell does he need a refresher on what the rest of the world is up to?"

"I dunno," Stanley said. "Unless Gelson intends being number one."

"How does he do that?" Adams said.

"Well," said Stanley, "that file lists all the world psychics, past and present, and their work in progress or done. It gives names, you see. All Gelson has to do now is pick them all off one by one, and he's got it."

Adams frowned. "Got what?"

Stanley shrugged. "Control of the psychic phenomena world."

"Sonofabitch," Adams said. "You got any idea on who'd get his attention first?"

"No, sir."

The man from National Security cleared his throat.

"What have you got to say, Cantrell?" Adams said.

"Our department is of a differing view, sir. We are of the opinion Gelson has been heisted. Picked up by another power."

"Any idea which one?"

"No, sir," Cantrell said. "A bit too soon to make any sound judgments."

"That's really great," Adams said. "I like the way you fellows work."

"It figured somebody would grab him anyway, if he didn't go over to them voluntarily."

"How's that?" Adams said.

"You didn't give him the piece of paper."

"What piece of paper?"

"What he asked for at the beginning. Something to protect him in the event he wasn't successful in the Federal Building and got picked up."

"That's tough shit," Adams said. "It's the way we work. We don't need any half-assed entertainer psychic telling us how to run our deployment ops."

"Maybe not. What do we do now?"

Adams shrugged. "Get Joe Polo."

The man from Security hesitated. "Polo? You sure you want him?"

"Of course, I'm sure," Adams said. "He's our most effective counter-spy and assassin, isn't he?"

"That's just the point, sir. We're all familiar with how Mr. Polo works. He kills first and asks questions afterwards."

"So?" Adams said coldly.

"In a case like this, Joe Polo might decide to keep matters simple by killing Gelson. I mean, to keep him from working for the other power."

"Okay," Adams said. "What about it?"

"I thought we had a higher stake in this. That the idea was to get Mr. Gelson back so that he could work for us."

Adams looked down his long aristocratic nose. "Whatever gave you that idea, Cantrell?"

Cantrell rubbed his jaw. "Well, maybe I didn't

28

hear everything," he remarked.

"What's your point, Cantrell?"

"Simply that I think Gelson and his kind of power is too valuable. He's more valuable to us alive than dead."

Adams shrugged. "Okay. When you get hold of Joe Polo, try telling him that."

Cantrell jutted his jaw and looked stern. "If Polo works for us, he damn better take orders from us."

"Fine," Adams said. "You tell him that, too."

Joe Polo climbed out of the pool behind the beachhouse in Malibu shedding water and picked up the phone. "Polo here," he said squinting into the hot California sun.

"This is Cantrell."

"Oh, Jesus," Polo said. "Have a heart. I'm just learning to walk again."

"This should be easy. Just hop into your car and meet me at the Airport Hotel. I'll be sitting around the pool."

Polo frowned. "This better be important. I'm still on sick leave."

"It's important enough to make me fly out to talk to you."

"Okay. Give me an hour." He hung up swearing, tossed a towel over his bulky shoulders, and headed for the house. He showered, slipped into jeans and a sport shirt, fitted his bare feet into sandals, and walked toward the carport and his car with a slight limp.

Traffic was light on the Coast Highway and he made good time. It had to be damn important for Cantrell to come out himself. A phone call from that department meant trouble, Polo knew, but he hadn't heard of anything going on lately that needed his personal skills.

He looked at himself in the rear view mirror wondering if Cantrell could tell he'd been hitting the bottle kind of hard after the last caper—when a .38 piece of hot lead had just missed his favorite fun area and damaged his thigh muscle instead.

It had been a rough trip into the mountains beyond Guadalajara where the local bandidos were holding Professor Emil Klugherz hostage. They wanted $50 million for the professor who didn't look nearly worth it to Joe Polo. But State said he was important, an archeologist who had spent nearly all his life in Mexico finding lost villages and temples, and in the process learned more secret paths through the jungles than the natives knew themselves. Until State had all Professor Klugherz's map network in their files, they needed him in the event of 'national emergency.'

Polo did his job, killed a lot of bandidos, and got shot up himself, but brought the old man out of there and delivered him safely to an aide of Cantrell. He got twenty-five thousand for the job and thought it little enough. Considering what his life might have been if the bullet had hit a few inches higher, he should have asked for a million, he told himself.

He had stayed in the sun the past month since, knitting and healing, and he was getting restless for some action again. He hated Cantrell's guts, as he did Stanley's and the other assholes always at him with smart tricks to pull off. But the money was good and always on the line, and Polo shrugged his powerful shoulders. What the hell else was a man supposed to do but put his life on the line doing his job?

The women he met along the way were spectacular, too, and Joe Polo grinned sardonically, never a man to neglect smelling the roses along the way.

Cantrell was too anxious to brief him about the Gelson disappearance to go into his drinking habits. "We figure we can go thirty if you return Mr. Gelson in good condition."

"Who's got him?"

Cantrell shook his head. "We don't have that information."

Joe Polo stared. "You want me to work blind for a lousy thirty thousand? A man like that could be anywhere in the world by now."

"It's only twenty-four hours," Cantrell said. "He also could be holed up here somewhere. State is also considering the possibility that Mr. Gelson has abducted himself with the general idea in view of working up his own business."

"I hope he makes it," Polo said. "Meanwhile I'm asking for fifty big ones."

Cantrell pouted. "Isn't that a little steep?"

Polo shrugged. "You're forgetting one thing. Supposing I find your missing Gelson, and he doesn't appreciate the idea. He stops clocks, doesn't he?"

Cantrell nodded sourly. "So what?"

Polo patted himself tenderly. "I just had a real close call down in Mexico. I wouldn't want anybody to stop my clock."

Cantrell stood up. "I'll give them your terms. Remember, we want Mr. Gelson back in A-1 condition."

"Right on," Polo said. "But the sonofabitch better not try to put the whammy on me."

4

GELSON WOKE UP IN the back of a speeding sedan with two bulky men pinning him between them. He felt dizzy, his head hurt. He put his hand to the base of his skull and winced. He brought his hand back and saw it wasn't bloody, but wasn't too relieved, wondering if he perhaps had a concussion. He looked down at his empty hands and then between his feet. The bulky man on his right grinned and lifted the black attaché case.

"This?"

Guri nodded. "What's this all about? You people from Security? I can assure you I have—"

The man was shaking his head, the broad grin fixed on his face. Mongol features, thought Gelson. Slavic. He took a quick glance at the one on his left. Similar flat face with high cheekbones. The driver had a square neck, clean shaven, but looked the same stocky type.

"Russky?" Gelson asked.

His companions laughed and Gelson suddenly felt a chill of apprehension. Wasn't this the possibility that the man from State had mentioned? That other powers might be interested in getting his services? He felt for the tapes in his pockets and the man on his left saw him searching and grinned. He held up the spools for Guri to see.

"Oh, you got those, too?" Gelson said. "I'm afraid they won't be much good to you now. Tapes do funny things with me around because of this strange power—" He stopped short. His head hurt him and he wondered if he could do anything with that kind of king-size headache going. One of the men in the back said something to the driver and when he turned barking a gutteral response, Gelson sucked his breath in sharply.

The driver was Chinese.

It didn't make sense at all now to think these men were from U.S. Security, picking him up for rifling their Air Force vaults. The two look-alikes in the rear with their Slavic features and the man in front, a slant-eyed giant Chinese, altered his conception of the situation. He realized too, whatever the man in the rear had said was in a language he didn't understand, no more than he did the response of the driver.

That's great, he thought, really terrific. My first assignment as a volunteer spy and I wind up with the wrong government. Aloud, he said to the men, "Who are you? Where are you taking me?"

The heavy-set man on his right shook his head.

"No talk now. You find out."

"I think you're making a big mistake," Gelson said. "You got the wrong man. My name is Gelson. Are you sure I'm the one you wanted?"

The man on his right grinned. "No worry. You see pretty quick."

The car turned to an on-ramp and went on the freeway heading south. Mexico? Gelson thought. A ship in San Diego and off to South America, and then flown to China, Siberia—? He shook his head and winced again at the pain. There had to be something he could do. Why give in to these paid assassins? Hadn't Adams been totally impressed with his powers? Wanted to hire him for the government, he had said. Well, then, he thought, let's make believe the situation is real. You're an impossible spy caught up in an even more impossible situation.

All right, Gelson, you got the powers. Let's see you use them and get out of this mess.

He had frozen the heavy elevator motor, he remembered. Why not the car? It didn't have to be any particular part, just let a piece of metal fall off. That would be a start.

Guri concentrated. His head ached and he couldn't get the intense feeling he wanted. He closed his eyes. Right wheel . . . fall off, he commanded mentally.

Another part of him shrilled inside. Hey, you crazy? At seventy miles an hour you want a wheel to come off?

Okay, forget the wheel. Something else.

Like what? another questioning self demanded.

The engine, maybe, he thought. Let a piece fall off the engine. Lots of metal there. Pistons, rods, fan belt—be my guest.

He tried projecting a thought toward the engine, but his head felt weak and giddy. No power there. No nothing. Maybe these dumb apes ruined his head, ruined his talent forever. He never knew exactly how it worked, but concentrating hard was always a big part of the deal, and for that he always assumed you needed a sound head.

Metal, metal, he repeated mentally. Something's gotta be metal I can reach.

His eyes focussed on the front part of the car, toward the ignition key, but the huge bulk of the driver appeared to thwart him. That solid thick neck was a beefy column of bone and muscle intercepting anything he could pass mentally. The huge shoulders squarely in front of him nearly filled the entire front seat of the speeding car.

Gelson knew the men on either side of him carried guns. He could see the bulky outline in their lapels, and when one of them turned, he saw the black grip of the automatic. Gotta be a forty-four or forty-five, Gurl, he told himself. No way you're going to bend them.

His eyes squinted bleakly out the windows. Traffic was still light on the freeway going south. Going north, he saw a black and white patrol car leading a pack of irritated drivers at the slow legal speed of 55 mph.

The idea struck him immediately. Lunatic maybe, but feasible. Okay, so be it, he said to himself, let there be a speed cop behind us, let our driver be heavy-footed, hitting the pedal to the floor, and then the motorcycle cop comes—

Cars whizzed by from the opposite direction. Was he imagining things or where they going faster? He couldn't see the speedometer. The driver sat squarely erect at the wheel. Driving fast wasn't that complicated.

Then incredulously, he heard the siren coming

from far back and turning his head quickly before the others, he saw the blinking red light. The driver too heard it before the others in the back seat, and Guri saw him glance into his rear mirror with a grimace on his stolid square face.

"Fuzz, guys," Guri said to their perplexed faces as the driver slowed.

In seconds, the siren was wailing in their ear and the speedcop was at their shoulder, then abreast of the driver thumbing him in toward the rail.

The driver said something in their special language to the men in the rear, and they cursed him. He shrugged and braked and the car turned out of its lane and came to a stop at the inside railing.

The cop was off his bike and striding toward them, gun on his hip. Guri leaned forward and as the cop stuck his face in the window, said, "Well, thanks a lot, guys. I can walk the rest of the way."

"I'm Rita Quimby," the girl said. "They say I should talk to you. What's this all about?"

"My name is Polo," he said. Looking her over, he saw a nice-looking blonde with cropped hair. Slender waist, good breasts. Shapely tan legs under the short flared skirt. She looked to be about twenty-four. "Are you with the Air Force?" he said, "I mean, in it?"

"No. Civilian worker. I'm with computer data."

Joe Polo looked around the large office. There were as many service people as civilians at their desks, walking around. "I'm investigating a disappearance. Any place we can talk?"

The girl shrugged. "There's a cafeteria downstairs."

"How long can you take?"

"As long as you need me. Colonel Pyne said I was to give you any assistance I could."

Joe Polo grinned. "Well, let's try the coffee, for openers."

As they walked out of the room, she said, "I understand it's about that, er, strange young man who visited us the other day."

"Right, miss. And anything you can remember about him will help. Anything at all. I'm starting from scratch."

They were in the long hallway now heading toward the elevators. "Well, here was where the first strange thing happened," she said. "The elevator doors were open. That was odd enough because they weren't on *hold*. I pressed the down button but nothing happened. The doors remained open. Car didn't move."

She pressed the red button on the wall and a moment later the car with the red light above it stopped and the door swished open. They stepped inside. As she raised her hand, Polo said, "Hold it, please. Don't do anything."

She looked surprised, but obeyed. The door closed behind them as they stepped into the car. The car hung there. Polo pressed the button to the floor and the door flicked open. He waited and the door closed. "Everything seems to be working fine," he said.

She smiled, showing large even white teeth. "They said it was the first time anything ever went wrong with the controls since they put up this building."

Polo nodded. "Okay. Take it from the other day."

She explained how the man moved his hands as they went in and the door closed. "I pressed the lobby button and nothing happened. The door was open then. But he looked at me and said, 'Allow me.' Then he passed his hands over the buttons. He said something like, 'Abacadabra and all that. The girl wants coffee. Let's go already.' The door closed and down we went. I didn't think anything of it at the time. Not until I found out who had done the trick."

Joe Polo nodded. "Guri Gelson. So according to you, he can stop an elevator and make it start by moving his hands—"

"He used a magic word. Abacadabra."

Polo grinned. "Yeah, but I think we both agree he didn't need it. He was just giving it kind of a touch, you know?"

"That's right, Mr. Polo. He said something like how he likes to show off."

"Did he say anything else?"

"He asked me the time."

"Remember what it was?"

"Ten-thirty-eight—I told him."

Joe Polo rubbed his chin. "Funny. The guards downstairs both had the same times as when he came in—10:08—so it would appear Mr. Gelson stopped their watches and let yours alone."

"Well, he was awfully nice and polite. He didn't have anything to fear from me. The guards—well, I imagine he had to do something to them."

"Sure, but Jesus! How can he do those things? Both saw him. Neither can remember what he looked like. One guy was face to face. He said all he could remember was thinking of his childhood. Happy times. That Gelson made him feel good."

The car door swished open and they stepped into the big marble lobby. "That's not so bad," she said. "Making a person feel good."

"I agree. Only what he did to those files upstairs is something else again. Where do we get the coffee?"

Joe Polo followed her down the corridor to the glass doors. The cafeteria was large enough to feed the entire building and they found a table off to the side overlooking the parking lot. "You went down to the lobby floor with Gelson but he stayed inside the car?" Polo asked.

"Yes. I stepped out thinking he was coming. But instead he waved good-bye. The door closed. The red light over the elevator stayed on and I assumed he went down to the basement. The security guards figured the same thing. By the time they got down there, he had disappeared."

Joe Polo looked moodily out the window to the big lot. "The basement door leads to that parking lot. Gelson comes out. Nobody stops him. He gets into his car and drives away."

Rita Quimby looked into the agent's gray eyes. "But where would he drive to?"

Joe Polo pushed his coffee cup away and lit a cigarette. "That's the million-dollar question, Miss Quimby. Does he take the stuff back to his pad, go to a previously selected hideout, or does he drive south to Mexico and get out of the country?"

"Why would he do that? I mean, leave the country? Didn't you say this job he did was a test with the permission of the State higher-ups, to find out what kind of spy Gelson would make?"

"Yeah. Only they're too chicken to admit it. How the hell can you not want a man like that to work on your side? If he can mentally stop elevators from moving, can you imagine what else he could do?"

"I hadn't thought much about it," the girl said. "A lot, I suppose. But he didn't give off any aura like that at all. He just seemed to be a pleasant-faced young man, with dark eyes. Very tan. An alertness to his expression. He seemed actually to be very good-natured."

Polo watched his hand descend and hit the plastic-topped cafeteria table. "I hope to hell he stays good-natured. I'd hate to think of some of the terrible things that man might do if somebody got him mad."

The girl nodded. "There's something you haven't mentioned. I've read quite a lot of spy stories and seen the films. What of the possibility that some other power, other than the U.S., has him. Let's say, some unfriendly power."

Polo got redder in the face. "I like the way you do my thinking for me. That's the big worry, of course. And after you reach that, all you have to worry about is who's the lucky one to get him?"

5

GELSON SMILED REMEMBERING the dumfounded looks of the beefy men in the sedan when he ducked through the door, excusing himself. The California Highway patrolman in blue with white helmet was holding his hand out for the driver's license.

"Sock it to them," Guri said. "Personally, I think they all had too much to drink."

The motorcycle cop didn't do anything more alarming than scowl. He made no mention of the illegality of pedestrians on the freeway, and Guri made his way along the inner rail until he came to the downramp. There were patches of grass on the other side and he wanted to jump but his head throbbed too much to try it.

There was nothing to do now, he thought, but get back to his apartment and wait for Cantrell's men from State Security. He looked at the sign over the downramp. El Segundo. Not too bad. There was a bus running along Sepulveda, the surface street, and if he got tired of waiting, he could always flag a lift.

He stumbled along, feeling giddy and rocky, his vision not too clear, when he got to the street. He wondered briefly who the donkeys were in the sedan and why they had tried to abduct him. Russia or China, he thought. Adams or Cantrell had spoken of the possibility of foreign powers being interested in him.

Their attempt couldn't have been too serious, or they would have killed the bike cop. But his throbbing head reminded him it nearly had been serious enough. He would have to wait till he got back to his pad before trying a few easy things. If his power was knocked out, it would all be a different kind of ballgame for him. No more show biz. No TV and Johnny Carson or Merv. His tan face wore a worried set. He hadn't thought of this for a long time.

What the hell was he going to be when he grew up?

They had never made anything clear. Just given him the secret whammo power. Bend the spoons, fix the clocks, open locks, Guri. We'll tell you some day what it all means.

And what if they don't, he thought again, then what happens? I stick with the entertainment, stay with Sam Pine and let him book the act. Maybe by the time I play the Palladium, I'll be able to do the important things.

The bus came along and Guri got on. He never

saw the dark sedan come slowly off the freeway and trail the streets looking for him.

An hour later, he was walking up the steps of his apartment in Santa Monica. There weren't any strange or sinister men lurking downstairs. No dangerous hardware levelled at him. Guri shrugged. Cantrell had said his men would be along to pick him up. Maybe he could lie down upstairs in his room until they arrived. They'd bitch about the missing tapes, he thought, and then grimaced. Screw them! He had stuck his neck out for the bastards, and all he had was a sore head to show for it.

He came in dog-tired, beat from the sun, his skull busy announcing a king-size headache. Too nauseated to eat, Guri stumbled into his bedroom. It was dark, reasonably cool, and quiet. He stretched himself out on the bed, closed his eyes and fell asleep.

Rita Quimby said good-bye to Joe Polo, wondering if she would ever see him again. His tough hard looks and bulky shoulders appealed to her. She had worked for the Air Force for three years in her capacity as computer data technician. The farthest thing from her mind was the chance that she would ever in real life meet a secret agent.

Joe Polo—the name fit him, she thought. Down to earth, seemingly ordinary, the common man. Only the glint in his eye and the tight jutting jaw conveyed the purpose of the man. Then when you took in the rest of him, the broad shoulders, deep chest, large sinewy hands, you had to acknowledge this could be a formidable fighting machine.

She didn't know how many men Polo had killed in line of duty. Officially, it was in double numbers. But there was also a considerable number Joe Polo had dealt with on his own, for purposes of his own, privately. If she had asked him about this, he probably would have shaken his head, unable himself to recall. There were things that a man had to do, and he did them.

The task he had, of finding Gelson, seemed to her an impossible one. The many spy stories and war films she had seen had conditioned her to the extremes of horror, the sadistic impossible roles of cruel ambitious men ruthlessly bidding for power. Besides the new atomic weapons, she knew of the deadly discoveries in chemical and bio warfare. Recently, she had processed the input of a research lab report on the mechanisms behind biofeedback, mental torsion, and aversion techniques.

A man with Guri Gelson's unexplainable energy output, that could wreck metals and deflect electronic waves, could easily be the most important potential spy ever captured. She ran down the long list in her head of the many countries, developed or not, which might be able to use Gelson one way or another, and how; and she sat shaken. The possibilities were seemingly as endless as his potential kidnappers.

If any of the big powers got him, certainly he could be used as a threat, a deterrent to any ongoing policies that a particular government had certain resistance toward. Russia, China, France —all could use him. Great Britain was a dim possibility but then, what if he were in the hands of the Irish fanatics? The developing black countries in Africa? Portugal, Spain, Egypt—the Palestine Liberation Army?

She sat at her desk, head spinning as she envisaged Gelson entrapped in some network of foreign deviltry, brainwashed, perhaps drugged, helpless to do nothing but obey his new master.

Rita had been given the story from Joe Polo as he understood it from Cantrell, the man from National Security. About how the Gelson effect at the Federal Building had been a planned dry run, to test out what he could do. That it had somehow backfired pleased Rita Quimby, but she thought about the nice young man with the odd sense of humor in the elevator, and she worried about him.

His fame as an entertainer had still not been strong enough for her to have recognized him, but her friends had seen him perform on the Carson show and with Merv. They all swore to the same story— Gelson had asked his audience to put their silverware out in front of the TV set, and also to trot out any broken clocks or watches, vacuum cleaners or jewelry, rings, keys, locks. He had declared that he would mentally will the metal objects to bend, the broken machines to repair themselves, and certain pieces of jewelry to disappear completely from the sight of the viewers.

That said, he had sat back in his chair next to the talk show host, closed his eyes, and in a soft relaxed voice had murmured: "All right, you things out there. Do what I want you to do. I want all you spoons to bend, also you keys and rings. I want every watch and clock that's been broken to pay special attention, because when I count to three, I want you all in perfect running order. Okay, you all got the message? Here we go now—one, two, and a-three—"

They had all screamed in her house, her friend said, and especially when the teapot sailed up off the table, moved to the other side of the room and waited until a kitchen cabinet door opened for it before it floated inside. They had five spoons bent nearly double, two keys, a ring and a screw-driver. Her dad's watch that hadn't run in over fifteen years began to tick again, and the vacuum cleaner they had given up for dead had suddenly roared to life and begun moving around the carpet.

"I don't believe it," Rita had said.

"You better, because I saw it with my own eyes," her friend told her. "And don't forget this was an earlier show—taped hours ago, coming from Vegas, over 500 miles away. Over the mountains. down the valleys, down the canyons and right into West Los Angeles and through our living room set. I nearly fainted."

Rita had heard it from others since and had resolved to personally witness the next Guri Gelson appearance. But now she smiled, realizing she had seen him in one of his better off-camera moments, doing that little trick with the elevator, keeping it nice and cool, closing the door for her with a nice flourish and the magic word all kids are brought up to know—abacadabra!

She worried so much now that she decided to take the day off. Colonel Pyne wouldn't mind, she thought. knowing she was the darling of his most secret dreams, unavailable to the old chap, but then even the military could live in hope.

As she left the Federal Building, she had the oddest notion that Gelson was calling for her.

Rita Quimby got into her red Mustang with-out any idea of where he lived nor where he was. But as she swung out of the lot into Veteran Avenue, something inside her head clicked and told her to head west. She turned west on Wil-shire and the beam in her head told her she was doing fine. She was nearing the last few remaining streets, before the broad boulevard ended with the Pacific below the cliff edge, when the beam picked her up again and told her to go left at the next corner. She turned, and was hardly into the second pick-up gear when the direction came again.

This time it told her to stop and she obeyed, swinging in close to the curb. Low two- and three-storied apartment houses dotted the street. Now what? she asked silently, and receiving no answer got out of her car and stood on the walk. It would be crazy, utter madness to go up and down the street looking for the missing psychic. Then she smiled, remembering there were telephone books listing names and addresses, and perhaps Mr. Gelson was so listed.

As she turned, an unseen force seemed to stop her, barring another step. She turned left and was now facing a gray two-storied building. Shrugging her slim shoulders, she went up the few steps. There was a small hallway with mailboxes and she was ready to scream inwardly with excitement when she saw the name GELSON in the mailbox slot.

She went upstairs to apartment No. 3, knocked on the door. Nobody answered, and she took a deep breath and turned the knob.

"Took you long enough to get here," he growled.

She stared, shook her head wonderingly, and stepped into the living room. She closed the door behind her and stood for a moment, leaning back against it, her heart beating fast, not at all certain how this had happened to her.

Gelson was sitting in a deep chair, a towel folded upon his head. "Do me a favor and put some ice on this, Quimby," he said. "I got this rotten headache that's killing me."

She took the damp towel off, saw the blood caked on it and said, "What happened to you?"

He shrugged, eyes half-closed. "A couple of dumb hitmen jumped me when I left your building. They were taking me someplace south in their car when I managed to get away."

Rita nodded, eyes staring. "But how did you manage to get me here? How did you know my name?"

"You bring the ice in the towel, I'll tell you."

She brought it back, arranged it on his head to cover the swelling. "Mr. Gelson, I think you should know something."

He put a tan hand to his head. "I know, I know. I'm a much wanted, very desirable psychic commodity. So what else is new?"

"How did you know my name?"

"You were wearing the name badge when you came out of your office the other day. That's why I concentrated on bringing you out here. You're one of the few names I can remember since I was hit. So I figured maybe you could do something here."

She tensed suddenly. "Wait a minute. I thought it was my idea to take the rest of the day off. But it was really yours, wasn't it?"

Guri shrugged. "Not too tough a trick. I just thought it would be nice to talk to you, find out what's been going on, and after that, it all seems to be pretty much mechanical." He flashed a sudden grin. "Find it all right?"

She nodded. "As if I were on a beam. Radar, or whatever. That's an incredible thing, really."

He groaned. "Not really. The incredible thing is now about to happen."

Her eyes widened. "What do you mean?"

48

He gestured toward the door. She turned to face it and saw it open and three men walk inside. They were dressed well, neat and hard-looking. They were well-armed, too, Rita noticed.

"Ask them if they're the guys from State," Gelson said.

The center man grinned crookedly. "Tell him to guess again."

. . . 6

THE CENTER MAN WALKED toward them smiling.
He had pale blue eyes and light blond hair closely
trimmed. The automatic he held stiffly in front
of him seemed outrageously large, Rita decided.
The gun lifted and she thought, what's all this
about? There was a puff of smoke and the scent
of something bitter-sweet around her.

She looked down and Guri Gelson seemed to be
coughing. She heard the coughing as a kind of
muffled sound. There was a soft wind in her ears
and then the room began to spin around her. She
looked for Gelson but couldn't see him. She closed
her eyes thinking she would try to look for him
later, and then forgot about it.

Rita felt a soft thud and saw the carpet near her face. There were more people in the room now, and two of them seemed to be wearing white, looking like nurses. I wonder who's sick? Rita thought, and her eyes closed and she fell asleep.

Gelson watched her fall, his mind detached. He had picked up a warning signal that these visitors would be bad for him, but there was no way he could avoid the strange-smelling gas. Nerve gas, he thought, probably harmless, and fell off his chair.

He felt something being thrown over him and then he had the odd sensation of floating out the door. His eyes flicked open and were dazzled by bright sunlight. He saw a gray car in the alley carport. Two men were in the front seat. Gelson closed his eyes and gave himself up to the power of the nerve gas.

It wasn't until a few hours later that Joe Polo came to the scene. He saw the two men parked in the carport also and looked closer. They were sitting in oddly transfixed positions but once he saw the neat small bullet holes between their eyes, Polo knew the two special agents Cantrell and Security had sent to cover Gelson were dead.

He went upstairs to the vacant apartment and found strips of adhesive tape and a strange odor close to the carpet. He knew the stuff well and threw the windows open. There were no signs of violence and apparently Gelson had been taken without a struggle. The pellet of gas could have done the trick, Polo knew, and then as he went for the telephone, he saw the purse. There was no identification in her bag, leaving it strictly up to him to guess who the female caller was.

Gelson had returned, from wherever he had

been after busting the Federal Building, and been taken quickly afterward. The odor of the gas in the room was so faint, Polo estimated the snatch at about noon. Not a bad trick for that time of day.

There was a sound downstairs near the landing and Polo put down the phone softly. He went to the window overlooking the street and saw a long dark green sedan at the curb. He came away from the window, and when he heard the sound of padding feet coming up the stone steps, he slipped behind the front door, leaving it purposely open a few inches.

He waited out of sight until the three bulky big men had entered the room. They spoke quickly to each other in harsh gutteral sounds he knew as Russian. They smelled the gas too and apparently knew almost without looking that Gelson was gone. They were turning to go, when one of them spotted the girl's purse.

For some reason, this triggered Joe Polo, and he had his Special Agent Colt .38 out and on a straight line, calling to them to drop it and spitting flame when they reached for their own weapons.

One had a Luger, the other a Mauser, and the third, the fast Beretta M 70 S. But Joe Polo was in a crouch, in the shadowy corner, the advantage clearly his, shooting into big targets outlined against the morning light. Each Russian agent got off a shot, and each received two in exchange. The difference was mainly that Joe Polo put each of his two shots within an inch centering on the chest area, and the men from Moscow had each been hit once and their firing was merely a reflex and wild.

Joe Polo came out of his crouch then, put in a

new load and went across the room for a closer look. They were all nicely dead, no kicking around, or bits of skull and brain tissue staining the walls. A good kill, and Polo went through their pockets, picked up the phone and told the local CIA contact man what he would find when he got over.

Kills had to be confirmed and accounted for, otherwise the bookkeeping would be a mess, Polo knew, and at his rates Cantrell, Stanley, and Adams always had to be reassured as to his continuing success. There were always arguments about his scale and hard discussions on how best to accommodate both his sense of justice and the government's. There was a time he had a flat going price of a thousand dollars a day, and then it went up to five, and some smartass accountant at State said that was rather high.

They had discussed a going rate of so much a kill, so much more for important people; but then knowing Polo had no conscience and might be willing to kill even his own mother, if he had one, for an extra five grand, they let that policy drop, too. The current rate was the highest known to the department, and Polo grinned going out the door, figuring he had given the bastards a good opening for his money.

He would have to kill a good many more, he figured, before he got Gelson away from whoever had him—and the girl, whoever she was, as well. Probably he might get his own head blown off this time, and Polo thought about that, didn't care much for the idea, and went out nervously looking for more trouble.

Polo went back to the car with the two dead agents and checked their billfolds. Casper was thirty-four, with the department thirteen years.

Huff was twenty-nine, and a comparative new-comer, a five-year man. Polo studied the bullet holes in their heads. Ballistics alone could identify the guns, but the holes were small enough to be .22 caliber. A killer using a weapon that small had to be very certain of his skill. They had been shot less than three hours before he got there, he estimated.

He checked the ground for possible clues, and the car itself. The killers had to be daring to have attempted this kind of snatch, a man and a girl, at midday in a fairly lively neighborhood.

Finding nothing, he went next door. He got lucky at the first ring. The woman answering the door didn't remember hearing any shots or loud noises. She had her TV set on all day, she explained. Polo smiled to himself. He had fired six shots and the Moscow men three. That should have alerted somebody. But oddly she remembered the wailing sound of a siren earlier and had gone to her window to see an ambulance parked outside next door.

Polo asked if she knew Gelson and the woman said she hardly ever got out and knew nobody in the neighborhood. He thanked her and left. The ambulance suggested an old bit, an easy way to smuggle a body aboard a plane. It had been done many times before and was always good for sudden departures with wanted subjects. They would generally be heavily bandaged and taped, altogether unrecognizable, attended by spurious doctors or nurses.

It was routine then to check all the airports for overseas flights, alerting the border patrols. Nothing untoward was reported. No passengers departing in stretchers, disguised or visibly under the weather.

Polo went back to his Malibu beachhouse to brood about the disappearance of Guri Gelson and the woman, and await developments. Whoever had the prize psychic would be heard from soon.

Cantrell called him at midnight. "We've been informed Mr. Gelson is safe and well and in good hands. Also some girl. I don't quite understand that."

"She was visiting Gelson, and taken along. All right, Cantrell, let's cut the crap—who has him?"

"He sounds definitely paranoid."

"Did you say *he*? I thought we were talking about *they*?"

"It's a he. Some power-crazy megalomaniac."

Joe Polo sighed heavily. "You're saying that it's not some country? That it's an individual—a single person?"

"That's the information we are going on."

"Christ," Polo said disgustedly. "You mean this was just an ordinary heist—a bleeping kidnapping?"

"Well, a bit more than that actually. There is a rather large implied threat along with the offer, as you might guess."

Joe Polo took his Colt .38 out and wagged it at the phone. He gladly would have shot Cantrell's flapping lips off. "What's the threat? What's the offer? And damn you, what's the name of whoever has him?"

"The threat is total destruction of our West Coast cities, starting with San Francisco, then Los Angeles, and finally the capitol at Sacramento. The ransom offer is a mere one hundred billion dollars in gold—and I'm not altogether certain there's that much in the world, but he's willing to discuss that. To negotiate, as he put it."

"That's just great," Polo snarled.

"The individual responsible owes no allegiance to anybody, apparently. He is his own man, perhaps leader of his own organization. I've never heard of him, and doubt that you have, Polo, despite your vast experience in the espionage field."

"Listen, Cantrell," Polo said. "I'm giving you five seconds to spill who the nut is. You stall me once more and I'll let you handle this spook yourself. The count is one, two, three—"

"Don't you be hysterical too," Cantrell said shrilly. "I've enough problems at this end. Adams expects me to take this threat seriously and—"

"Last chance, baby," Polo said.

"The name is Sanyo Zindel," Cantrell snapped.

"Say it again. Once more for the West Coast, sweetheart."

"Sanyo Zindel. Now don't tell me you've heard of him!"

"It just so happens, Cantrell. It just so happens. I've heard the name, and seen the man. You check over the list of scientists responsible for the first atomic bomb, and you'll see Zindel the first man fired from the project."

"Fired? Why?"

"I think he wanted full credit himself—instead of—what's his name—"

"Einstein?"

"No. Not Einstein . . . Oppenheimer! That was his name. Zindel claimed Oppenheimer stole one of his papers."

"Good Heavens, then he is mad!"

"Okay, now we both know. Tell me where the nut is and I'll see if I can flush him out."

"Well, he hasn't revealed that, yet. He's not

that stupid. But he's told us to keep a close watch on San Francisco as his first target for psychic phenomena fallout—his words, you understand."

"And you think he's bluffing?"

"Certainly. What can Gelson do for him up there that would be of any consequence to the rest of the country, or even of great damage to San Francisco itself? Bend some tablespoons, snap open a few locks on filing cabinets?" Cantrell brayed loudly, amused by his own wit.

"You know what I think, Cantrell? I think you forgot how to think—if you ever really knew. Don't you remember what Gelson did with the elevator in the Federal Building? Can you imagine what he can do with office building elevators in a city the size of San Francisco?"

"So?"

"Have you forgotten how he sent out thought waves from the Carson show and affected people and objects over 500 miles away? Jesus, that's just the beginning with Gelson! What do you do when he brings down aircraft and louses up radar?"

Cantrell was silent for a long moment. When he came on again, his voice was shocked, serious. "Surely you don't think Gelson would do—"

"Gelson is a prisoner. Pete's sake, Zindel knows enough about brainwashing technique to drive Gelson crazy enough to wipe out the entire country. Don't you realize yet he can do that? Anything metal he can affect. His thought waves can move objects, dematerialize them, I understand. He's got the kind of energy scientists still can't explain, don't you see? He's got the power only something from another planet can possibly have, because he's the only person living on earth who can do what he does." He let the words sink in before he went on.

"Don't you think Zindel is smart enough to realize his value?" Joe continued. "Don't you know Zindel can use Gelson as a weapon for bargaining with any country, any big power in the world?"

Cantrell cleared his throat. "Well, I hadn't taken the threat too seriously, but I will admit there is a certain bit of truth in what you're saying."

"Get with it, Cantrell," Polo said. "You better lay it on Adams, too, and all the other deadheads you're trying to have face for out there. What do you do, for example, if tomorrow Zindel makes Gelson offer you a sacrifice?"

"A sacrifice? What do you mean?"

"Let's say he brings down an airplane by extracting one small bit of metal it needs to stay aloft. Would that do it for you? Or maybe he crashes an elevator in an office building. Maybe he cuts off all the power and leaves the hospitals black."

Cantrell coughed. "You're being overly dramatic, Polo. We'll see what he has to say, and I daresay we can negotiate for Gelson for a considerably smaller amount without suffering any losses such as you mention."

"Then there's always the other possibility you jerks haven't thought of," Polo said.

"Such as?" Cantrell asked acidly.

"Like selling Gelson's services to any other power that wants him. You know, free lance. A job at a time. Playing one against the other. Let's say Egypt would want a little win over Israel—"

"Don't go away," Cantrell said. "I'll be getting back to you."

7

ZINDEL LOOKED THE KIND of man who had spent his youth picking wings off insects. You wouldn't have liked your sister going out with him, nor would you have elected to loan him money, or invite him over to a party. If you were a bank manager, you would have turned him down as a teller, and if you were a pilot you would have hoped somebody had checked the man's luggage.

There was something visibly reptilian and malignant about Sanyo Zindel. The large yellow spooky lizard-like unblinking eyes, thin bloodless lips, huge arched predatory nose. For the rest, what moved of his body was thin and scrawny, and his paralyzed and wasted torso sat encased in a powered wheelchair. His hands were pale white as was any visible skin, his shoulders thin and his chest sunken and narrow.

His head was larger than normal, and apparently his brain too; but somewhere along the line Zindel had developed obsessions too numerous to catalog—the prime motivating one, however, being that he was superior to the entire human race and that it owed him a long-term servitude. And as he was of a determined unforgiving nature, nothing could deflect him from what he considered to be rightfully his. That happened to be, for Zindel, the world.

He was trained as a physicist and biochemist, marine biologist, mathematician, electronics engineer, alchemist and astrologer. He had given up alchemy when one of his experiments had exploded and put him permanently into the wheelchair; but the accident merely served to nurture and further his hate against the world, and speeded his ultimate desire to make Sanyo Zindel the Number One man in the Universe.

Zindel spun his noiseless rubber-rimmed wheels forward to a low console with as many knobs and red-arrowed scopes and needles as any proper lift-off atomic missile site. He pressed a black button and an image appeared on the center home TV screen. "Send Gelson and the girl in," Zindel said.

The image nodded. It looked gray and tired and used to taking orders from the world's top egomaniac. "Yes, sir."

Zindel flipped the switch and an image on another screen appeared. "Report Z 1306!"

"One second, sir." The image was wearing a white asbestos lead-lined suit, a white hood of similar material with a plastic visor screen over the eyes. He consulted a long pad on a metal clipboard. "Laser control unsatisfactory at distance with penetration required. Multifeedback distortion presents dangerous possibilities for project condition."

Zindel nodded. "Stay with it. I want results. A definite affirmative result in three days."

The white image nodded. "Yes, sir. Will do."

"Is the mountain and its composition the drawback?"

"Yes, sir. The ray becomes blunted and fans out."

"Bend it, man. Distort the arc and go around."

Zindel switched off and pressed another lever allowing him to view another screen showing workers hosing down a missile site. "Attention!" Zindel said. "We'll have a test run to check out the circuitry at 1700 hours."

A heavy-set worker detached himself from the others and ventured toward a mike. "There is something wrong, sir. The electromagnetic frequency is changing faster than we can control it."

Zindel smiled. "Excellent! Exactly what I thought!"

The worker still was wearing a puzzled frown when his image was erased from the screen.

A door at the far end of the large laboratory opened. A gray-faced tired man appeared. "Yes, sir. You called."

Zindel swivelled around in his chair. "Where are they?"

The man blinked. "Where's who, sir?"

Zindel pounded the arm of his chair. "The girl, idiot, and Gelson. I sent you for them five minutes ago."

"Sorry, sir. I forgot."

He turned to leave and Zindel spoke. "Wait!" The man froze and Zindel propelled his chair toward him over the smooth floor surface. He looked up at the man, slack-jawed now, a vacant look in his eyes. "What did Gelson do to you, Bommer?"

The man shrugged, eyes puzzled. "Who, sir?"

Zindel sighed. "We have a man here with a girl. Please bring them here, Bommer. If he looks at you, cover your eyes."

The man nodded and went out the door. Zindel stared at the blank surface a moment. Then his eyes gleamed and he hit his palms together. "Fantastic! Even here as a prisoner he can exert his power. This may be the beginning of a new day for science!"

Meanwhile, Guri Gelson sat on a small chair in a large bare room looking up at a nervous girl. "What will happen now?" she said.

Gelson shrugged. He put a hand to the back of his head. "If this damn thing got better, maybe I could think. But whatever I try seems to fuse out."

"I'm not so sure," Rita said. "That man came here to do something with us. He seemed to forget what it was when you looked at him."

"I can't help that," Gelson said. "I've been trying to tell you. I don't understand this strange power I have. It seems to work sometimes when I try, when I concentrate. Then there are times when it's nothing. Like the battery is dead. Now when that man came here, all I was trying to do was find out what the head man wanted us here for. And all I got out of it was a strange word I never heard of."

"What was it?"

"It seemed like—looked like—*Zindel*. What could that be?"

She shook her head. "It couldn't be him. His name tag was Bommer. Don't you remember?"

62

"I didn't notice," Gelson said. "Do you have any idea where we are?"

Rita stared. "You mean you don't know, either?"

"Look," Gelson said impatiently. "You've got to bear in mind that apart from a few silly tricks I do, I'm really just a very normal guy. I inhaled the same kind of nerve gas you did, and when I woke up here, I was just as surprised as you. We were both unconscious since we were taken from my apartment. How in the world would I know where we are?"

"Okay, guess."

"An underground cave of some sort. Some vast subterranean hollowed surface, I guess. A lot of machinery around doing strange things, building, riveting, setting wires."

"That sounds like a pretty good guess," the girl said. "How do you know that?"

Guri grimaced. "I don't. All I have are these strange vibrations. And of course, the mental disturbances I always get when a lot of people are around. The machinery and wires—well, I can't explain that except anything metal sets up a sort of tingling in my hands."

"What about the hollow business. You said an underground cave?"

"I can't explain that, either. I just seem to sense great echo vibrations. And they're so far apart, it would indicate this place is larger than I would like to believe."

"I feel I've seen this movie somewhere. There's a mad scientist here who will want you to do something nasty for him."

Gelson clapped his hands. "That's right. His name is Zindel!" He blinked. "Haven't I heard that name before?"

"Don't worry about it. If it's something else, he'll correct you. What do you think will happen if you don't do as he says?"

"I don't know," Gelson said. "Remember, I'm just a very ordinary—"

The door opened and the man Bommer appeared. He put his hands over his eyes and said quickly. "Please follow me, the Master is waiting."

"What's his name, Bommer?" Rita said.

Bommer dropped his hand from his face and looked at Rita Quimby. "The Master's name? Zindel, of course. Sanyo Zindel. I thought everyone here knew."

"Look, Mr. Bommer," Guri said. "I don't know how much they pay you here . . . but I can get you a couple of free tickets to the Johnny Carson show—good for you and your wife—if you get us out of here."

Bommer covered his eyes again. "I'm afraid I can't help you there, sir. This, as you know, is a vast labyrinthine cave cut out of rock thousands of feet below the earth's surface. I've never been above, to my knowledge, since I came here. Will that be all, sir?"

Gelson stood up wearily. "No, Bommer. Take us to your leader."

They followed the slow-moving guide along a high narrow hallway, with pale stone walls along a stone-smoothed corridor, echoing with the clack of their heels.

"This place is beginning to look familiar," Rita said. "Early Flash Gordon. The Emperor Ming will be waiting in his throne room."

"Don't knock it," Guri said. "If this place is really underground, can you imagine the work that's gone into it? It's carved as carefully as the pyramids. There isn't a stone out of place."

"Naturally," the girl said. "Ming wouldn't permit it."

"Well, Miss Quimby," Gelson said, "if this chap Zindel fancies himself as Ming, we're in trouble. There's nothing I can do about stone walls. Except maybe beat my head against them."

The hallway turned and they followed the guide through a long maze of corridors. At the end of the final stretch was a large door. The guide knocked. "If you will enter, please."

The door opened and Gelson went through with the girl on his arm. Rita gasped. There was an eerie glow to the dark room, relieved by a circular window at the far end. A man sat motionless there in a steel wheelchair. As they drew closer, they could see the window was an aperture cut in a long tunnel, and at the far end, miles away they could see light and water.

The man in the chair nodded. His hand touched a lever on the arm of his battery-operated chair, and slowly and silently it moved toward them. Another fingertip motion and it stopped a few feet off. "I am Sanyo Zindel," the man said. His voice was soft, articulated clearly. "You are Mr. Guri Gelson, and this is—"

"Rita Quimby," the girl said. "And we're both waiting for an explanation. I hope you've got a good lawyer, Mr. Zindel, because when mine gets finished with you, you'll wish you hadn't read the Sunday funnies when you were a kid."

Zindel looked questioningly at Gelson.

"Miss Quimby thinks you're kind of far out here, Mr. Zindel. Like doing an old Flash Gordon bit, with yourself playing the Emperor Ming. You know, the arch enemy of civilization."

Zindel bowed from the waist to the girl, a fleeting smile crossing his harsh pale face. "Yes, I've read them, of course, Miss Quimby. There's one tremendous difference, you see. Flash and the Emperor Ming were comic creations, early attempts at science-fiction in the comic supplements. This is real. I am real. You are my prisoners, and that is real, also. As for my being the arch enemy of civilization, as you would have the Emperor Ming, I see it rather another way. That, more correctly, future ages may well consider me their savior."

"Oh, come on," Miss Quimby said. "I don't believe any of this. Maybe you're doing a new TV series, Mr. Zindel?"

"We'll leave it to Mr. Gelson," Zindel said. "He's a psychic. Ask him what is in my mind."

Gelson hesitated. He rubbed the back of his head gingerly. "Well, sure, I'm getting flashes. But there's something you oughtta know, Mr. Zindel. Before your troops came for me, I had a couple of other guys trying a heist. They hit me over the head right here—" He turned and bent at the waist so Zindel could see the bloody matted hair and the swelling bruise.

Zindel frowned. "Idiots. Your only strength and usefulness is the power of your mind. To think they would do that!"

Guri shrugged, straightening up. "I think maybe they were Russian agents. Anyway I got away and back to my joint where your own boys found me. But what I want to tell you, and I'm not kidding, is that my head isn't right yet. Maybe it will be, and then again maybe it won't." He smiled feebly. "I mean, I don't know exactly why you brought me here, but I can make a pretty good guess. And I just want you to know right off, before I even hear your proposition, that my head is damaged. If you don't wanna take my word for it, let your doctor look me over. I think maybe I got a concussion when that big ape creamed me."

Zindel smiled. "True, you are a bit off. But not as bad as you would think. You are operating within twenty percent of your former powers even now, Mr. Gelson, without your trying. Can you see that magnetometer on the console?"

Gelson and the girl looked at a wavering dial.

"The galvanic current is up since you stepped into the room." Zindel said. "We're in no hurry. We can wait till you heal."

Gelson looked pleased. "No kidding? Am I doing that?" He stepped closer to the console and the rising needle began to vibrate as it reached its highest mark on the scope.

"Careful," Zindel said. "Not too close!"

But Guri was leaning over the console fascinated by the effect his body magnetism and energy rays had on the meter. It whirled to the top, oscillated madly, then there was a sudden popping sound, the tinkle of broken glass and smoke came out of the console in a thin grayish swirl.

"Idiot!" Zindel was saying as he rushed his mechanical wheelchair forward. "Stand back! Dammit, now you've broken it!"

"Sorry," Gelson said, looking genuinely contrite and apologetic. "I wasn't even trying to do that. I was just wondering what time it was, and got to thinking about clocks—and well, you know, I got this thing where I can stop clocks, Mr. Zindel."

Zindel waved his hands at the smoke issuing out of the sleek console. "Do me a favor and go over there and sit down. I can see you're going to be a problem."

8

AT TWENTY-FIVE RITA QUIMBY was accustomed to dealing directly with any situation. She put her hands on her nice curving hips and faced Zindel. "Apart from your being utterly mad," she said. "Why have you brought us here?"

Zindel sighed. He knew a lot more about biochemistry and infrared and interstellar space, molecules and atomic fissions than he knew about women. "Mr. Gelson has been brought here for my own purposes. You happened to be there, and my agents decided to bring you along, as well. You serve no purpose here and as soon as Mr. Gelson agrees to my terms, you will be free to go, or otherwise as the situation permits."

"But what is he supposed to do? Surely you're not intending something ridiculous like intending to rule the world?"

"Oddly," Zindel said, "I think you've got it."

Rita stared, open-mouthed. "I was right. You are mad."

The renegade scientist shrugged scrawny shoulders. "Sticks and stones, Miss Quimby. If you and Mr. Gelson will look into the console for a few moments, I'll put the screens on view so that you can get a better idea on what's going on here. This isn't any impulsive cheap operation, you know. Look !"

As Zindel pressed the proper buttons, four small screens came up from black glass into instant focus. "From top left to right, those are the missile site and projectile, and the nuclear sub with SAM warheads. Range of 1,500 miles."

Gelson and Miss Quimby stared into the busy scenes.

"Lower left to lower right," Zindel said softly. "The tunnel through the last remaining mountain which will permit that strange-looking vehicle to move underground, crabwise, and topple tall buildings. It is atomic powered and laser armed. San Francisco will think it is having another earthquake. But we will know better, of course."

"San Francisco? Why San Francisco?" Rita said.

Zindel chuckled. "As the first mountaineer said, Miss Quimby, because it is there." He nodded to the screen on the lower right of the console. "That is another lab where we are testing subjects undergoing mind control. Biological psychology, mind alteration, biofeedback, neurological response to sensorimotor rhythms, operant conditioning—as you can guess, it is in that area where Mr. Gelson can do us the most good."

"How do you mean?" Rita said nervously.

"He can do all the things already we hope to program others to do years from now. Perhaps while he is here, we can learn his secret. Or again, perhaps he can demonstrate that with his particular and unique kind of mental energy, all these other operations, the missile and nuclear subs are so much junk, archaic ideas of control, subservient to Mr. Gelson's mind powers."

Rita smiled and tossed her head. "You'll find American boys don't brainwash that easily. You won't do what he wants, will you, Guri?"

Guri lifted his shoulders, rubbed his nose. "Well, I don't know. I don't know what he's getting at, Rita. I mean, if it's only an experiment—"

"Precisely," Zindel said. "From what I've observed, your full powers have yet to be tested. For example, I believe you don't know yet, that you have it within your power to bring any plane down from the sky just by thinking about it."

Guri blinked. "I do?"

Zindel nodded. "And not only planes, but since your energy waves distort radar, you can deflect any missile from its prearranged flight pattern."

Gelson stared. "I can?"

"Absolutely," Zindel said. "And with my own scientific methods of inquiry, far advanced in technology from those nitwits at UCLA, we can learn to utilize the strange currents which emanate from you, secrets only obtainable now— presumably—on some far-off planet."

"No kidding?" Guri said.

Rita shook her head. "Now wait just a minute,

Guri! Can't you see what he's doing? Feeding your ego? Don't listen to him. Don't forget I work for the U.S. Army Air Force and—"

Zindel's yellow eyes gleamed. "Ah!" he said, snapping his fingers. "So that's your connection!"

"I'm not in it," Rita said drily. ",Civilian personnel—I work for it."

"A very backward and reactionary group," Zindel said. "I did the same, at one time."

Rita stared. "You did? When?"

Zindel permitted himself a chuckle. "A while back. I was one of the group working on the Manhattan Project—"

"The first atomic bomb?"

"They cheated me out of it," Zindel said sullenly. "Perhaps if it weren't for Oppenheimer and Fermi, I might have received my proper credit."

"What did they have to do with it?"

"It was my theory first," Zindel said. "Oppenheimer stole my paper."

Rita edged away from the sallow scientist. Crazy, she thought. "And now you're getting even, right? You'll show them!"

Zindel shrugged. "That was the idea, at first. It's different now. I have a larger, more practical dream. It will become a reality with or without Mr. Gelson's aid. One way or another, I will rule the world."

Rita glanced at Guri and tapped her head significantly. "You better find yourself another line, Guri. You see what this all leads to?"

"Well, it does sound difficult," Guri said thoughtfully. "But when you consider the other possibilities, it might not be such a bad idea. I'd rather have a smart dependable person handling the world than a lot of stupid jerks driving everybody nuts."

Rita stared. "Are you saying you're going to work for him?" She thumbed a derisive gesture toward Zindel. "Where is your loyalty to your own country?"

Guri shook his head. "We're just talking, remember. I still haven't done anything. Anyway, if I did my thing for my own country, Adams would have wanted me to kill a lot of people too."

"Who's Adams?" she said.

"He works in the State Department. He wanted me to work for him, you know, after I did that Federal job."

"You're really dumber than I thought," Rita said hotly. "Do you really believe Mr. Zindel will let you go after you do some little trick for him?"

Guri looked surprised. "Of course. It's all just a big scientific test, isn't it?"

The girl looked at him and blew her cheeks out.

"Well, hardly, Mr. Gelson," Zindel said. "Miss Quimby is quite correct. Perhaps it's just as well that you understand your position here. In the first place, and I'm sure you will agree, you are a prisoner here, along with Miss Quimby of the Air Force."

"Hey, now wait," Gelson said. "She didn't do anything. I mean, what can she do to hurt you?"

Zindel stepped away to the console, shaking his head. A red light glowed on the panel board. "Send Felix in." He saw the inquiry in Rita's eye. "Felix is our resident monster."

The door opened at the east end of Zindel's room and a huge grotesque being plodded toward them. Zindel raised his left hand and the outsize

72

servitor veered toward Rita Quimby.

She stepped back, paling. "Guri, do something'"

He bit his lower lip, looking vexed and apologetic. "You got to remember, Rita, all I know how to do is bend nails, fix watches, bend keys —I don't know what to do here."

"Think," she said tartly. "Boggle his mind." Guri looked at the advancing creature. "All right, now," he said. "Cut that out!"

The shambling man kept coming.

Gelson shook his head. "I can't—my head hurts. Maybe later I'll think of something."

The monster was a man about seven feet tall and nearly as wide. At nodding signal from Zindel, he scooped Rita up in his arm. "Take her back to the room, Felix. And no funny business."

Rita screamed and pulled at the monster's shaggy hair. "Don't do that, Miss Quimby," Zindel said. "Felix will get very upset and tear you to little pieces."

As the shaggy thing carried her off, Rita wailed, "Guri! Do something."

"I'm sorry," he said. "You got to remember all I can do—"

"I know," she said. "Fix watches, bend nails, close elevator doors. Well, rotsa ruck with Emperor Ming."

As the monster carried her off, Zindel sighed. "She'll be fine, Mr. Gelson. Just as long as you cooperate."

Joe Polo got the call at 2:06 A.M. that night.

Cantrell spoke tersely. "We think we have a fix on him."

Polo yawned. "How about calling me back when you birds know for sure."

"No, no, listen to me," Cantrell said. "There's

a small island off San Francisco, near Tiburon, formerly used by the Coast Guard—"

"Angel Island, they call it," Polo said.

"Okay. Angel Island. Our radar station up at Fort Baker has been reporting a constant disturbance for the past twelve hours. Does that signify anything to you?"

"Not too much," Polo admitted. "Look, Cantrell, why don't you try me again when you know—"

"Now, look," Cantrell said heatedly. "You're supposed to be working for us. Our information is that this particular kind of radar distortion is quite unusual. It coincides with the odd energy ray output by Gelson—don't laugh—we've checked with the UCLA lab people who conducted the tests on him. Also it fits in with the time he's been missing. I'm of the opinion Gelson is trying somehow to transmit the exact position he is in. What do you think?"

Polo yawned prodigiously. "I think maybe this time you may have something, but only because it's all too ridiculous. Angel Island is a tourist attraction most of the time."

"Also," Cantrell said, "a Miss Rita Quimby has been reported missing. She works for the Army Air Force people in the Federal Building in West L.A. and—"

"I'm on my way," Polo said. "She was snatched with Gelson."

"Incidentally," Cantrell said, "are we to assume that the three Russian bodies at Gelson's apartment are yours?"

"Yeah," Polo said, "I phoned them in. Don't you guys even tell each other what's going on? Hey," he added, "have you turned up anything new since we last talked on Zindel?"

74

"Well, it seems you were quite right. He did work on the Manhattan Project of the atomic bomb. As for Oppenheimer having taken his paper, that's ridiculous."

"I know. But you'll agree what Zindel is up to now, isn't."

"We have a Coast Guard station near that island, Polo, if you require help."

"Keep them handy. I'd rather case the place myself. It may not be Gelson there anyway, you know. But keep with it. I want to know if Zindel intends carrying out his threat of knocking down San Francisco."

"Fine. Call me when you get up there. Perhaps I'll have heard from the gentleman."

"You don't know this guy. Gentleman he is not, pal." He hung up, feeling tense and alert, the way he liked to feel when he was onto something. He knew the area around the point of Tiburon and the small island. It had become so popular as a tourist attraction, they had run a ferry in from Fisherman's Wharf in San Francisco Bay.

He got into his car with his ready bag of armaments, and wheeled it to the airport. He made the next flight north with scant minutes to spare, having had to check with security before being allowed to board with his arsenal of guns and grenades.

A leggy airline hostess made the short flight tough for Polo because he still needed sack time, but she was blonde and very curvaceous, and probably meant it when she told him to look her up in San Francisco.

He rented a car at the airport and got a room at the small inconspicuous hotel he liked up the hill on Sutter. There wasn't any point to going off like gangbusters until he had spoken again with Cantrell. Polo downed a good part of the fifth of scotch he had picked up and settled into the king-sized bed.

Polo heard the noise roaring in his ears and thought it was part of a dream until his bed began shaking. Bits of plaster began falling from the ceiling and Polo remembered he was in Earthquake City and rolled out of the bed and hit the floor. He was on the eighth floor with several more above him, and he waited anxiously, but the first tremors had stopped and only the grinding noise continued. He got to the window and looked out. At first the glow in the sky puzzled him until he realized it was a fire at the west end down near Union Square.

People were opening windows in the apartment house across the street, sticking their necks out yelling. The streets were quiet. It was 5:05 A.M. and the city was still asleep. He heard the wailing sound of the fire engines then, and more sirens as the fuzz tore down the hills in their black and white patrol cars.

The phone in his room rang. It was Cantrell. "Zindel just called us. He said we could expect a demonstration early this morning as an indication of his plans."

"It's already happened, Cantrell."

"What? What the hell are you talking about?"

"Unless it happened to be an earthquake, it would seem Zindel—with perhaps the assistance of Mr. Guri Gelson—has knocked down the first target building in the Bay area."

"Good Heavens! What are you going to do about it, Polo?"

"First, I'm going to finish up my sack time. Then I'll call down for some breakfast. Then, if the elevator is still working, I'll go down to the water and find me a boat and see what I can do about it."

Cantrell was still talking, trying to impress upon him the extreme urgency of the situation when he hung up.

9

ZINDEL RUBBED HIS PALE thin hands together. "Well, Guri, shall we get down to work?"

Guri hesitated. "Gee, Mr. Zindel, I really don't know what to say. I mean, first I wanna know how's Miss Quimby in there alone with that Felix?"

"Tosh," Zindel said, waving his hand in dismissal. "Don't think about it. Worrying about a woman is one of the more serious forms of mental aberration, you know. Take it from me, none of them is worth the trouble."

"Well, I can appreciate your viewpoint, Mr. Zindel. But even though there's nothing serious between me and Rita, I'd still like to know for sure she's okay. You see, if she hadn't been trying to save me, she wouldn't be in this position. And she only got to my place because I directed her mentally to be there. So it would be all like kind of my fault if anything bad happens to her."

"Forget the girl, Gelson. We've got more important things to discuss. For example, I'd like your assistance in knocking down the Union Bank building in San Francisco."

Gelson stared. "Huh? What good would that do?"

"It would be a demonstration of our strength," Zindel said. "I've already warned the United States government of what I would do if it failed to comply with my demands."

"What demands?"

"I'm asking a hundred billion dollars for you. Naturally they won't pay it. And, consequently, that makes it only fair for me to carry out my immediate designs."

Gurl rubbed his head. His head still throbbed, but the pain seemed to be easing. "Oh, heck, I'm not worth that kind of money, Mr. Zindel. Nobody is. I thought you were going to do something good with me. You know, like maybe develop some new kind of energy power, so people could cut down on their light and gas bills, and so on."

Zindel stared. "This is no time to be naive, Gelson. I'm out for power—my own power. It's the government's worry to give them cheaper electricity, not mine."

"Well, there's other things. Like maybe curing sick people using my kind of energy. Like pulling their diseases out of them. Fixing headaches, cancer, tumors—like that. I always thought I'd like doing that. It sure would beat bending nails and spoons."

"Forget it, Gelson. You can't afford to dissipate your energies that way on that philanthropic nonsense. Now, come over here and I'll show you the plans to the Union Bank building. It's less than fifty miles away and would be a good starter for us."

Gelson shook his head firmly. He felt very disappointed in Zindel. "Gosh, no, I'm sorry, Mr. Zindel, but I'd rather not do anything like that. If it's all the same to you, I'm sorry you had to go to all that trouble, but I'd like to go home now. With Miss Quimby, of course."

Zindel's large oblate yellow lizard eyes widened. "What are you saying?"

"It wouldn't work out. I can't do anything bad with my gift. They wouldn't like it, you know."

"They? Who's they?"

Guri wagged his thumb upward. "You know, the cosmic powers who came down and gave the energy. If I did something wrong with it, they would take it away."

"Nonsense," Zindel said.

"You don't have to drive us all the way." Gelson said. "You can leave us out somewhere near a bus stop. Miss Quimby and I can get home from there. Or maybe we can hitchhike."

Zindel spun his wheelchair around to face Gelson squarely. "Yon don't understand your situation, Gelson. You're my prisoner and must do whatever I say. Don't you understand that? I'm not playing a game with you. You'll do as I say or I'll have to take steps to convince you I mean business."

Gelson looked puzzled. "But you can't do that, Mr. Zindel. I mean, I can't do any of my things unless I want to."

Wheeling to his console, Zindel pressed a button. "Let's find out about that."

Zindel's console glowed with an eerie phosphorescent light. A humming sound came from a hidden mechanism. Gelson cocked his head, wondering what this was all about. He really hadn't expected this kind of trouble with Zindel, and he hoped Zindel wouldn't be too angry. A recognized scientist with his know-how was the kind of man he had been hoping would take him over and help him get to know his inner powers, develop them so that they would be useful to humanity eventually. But he knew he was right in not going along, in refusing to permit his strange gift to be used for personal aggrandizement.

"Can you see this meter reading?" Zindel asked over his shoulder.

Gelson shook his head. He took a step over the grid-like floor to get a better angle and Zindel pressed another button. Gelson froze, a tremendous excitement gripping his body, an odd heavy feeling. He tried to move and couldn't. He tried to tell Zindel that something was wrong with his floor, that he ought to do something about this strange magnetic effect that was gripping his shoes and shaking him like a leaf in a storm.

Zindel turned to face him. "Don't worry about it, Gelson. It's only an anti-reticular system I've developed, which goes counter to normal arousal patterns. It is slowing down the brain waves from your cortex. In a few seconds, you won't have the energy to stand. A few more, and you will lose the energy to think or resist. When I want your cooperation, I'll send the waves in another direction. Meanwhile, rest comfortably, Gelson. I'll see you again when you're in a more agreeable frame of mind."

He reversed the switch, and Gelson toppled

over and lay on the grid floor, the muscles of his legs twitching. A door to the lab opened and a white-coated man entered. He walked directly to the fallen figure of Gelson, stopped and glanced at Zindel.

"Be careful with this one, Otto," Zindel said. "We will work on the parallel system of tranquillity with him."

The man's eyebrows raised. "The amygdala?"

Zindel nodded. "The amygdaloid nucleus has two major parts, the old and the new brain portions of the limbic system. We will bypass the hypothalamus with drugs and thus block any violent tendencies. I would say electrodes briefly in the left amygdala. Then slowly we will stimulate his brain with a weak electric current using the tip of the electrode until we find the exact spot where stimulation will reproduce the degree of compliance I shall need."

The other man bowed. "Very good, sir. I'll take him back with me then."

As Zindel nodded impatiently, the man stooped and propped the collapsed figure of Gelson to a sitting position. Then with a surprising show of dexterity and strength, he threw the young psychic across his shoulders and left the room.

Zindel frowned, rubbing his face with his thin sensitive fingers. What he was planning with Gelson was fairly common among neurosurgeons in their work on violent epileptics. They went further, injecting radiopaque dye to allow accurate Xrays of the brain following a hole drill-bored in the skull. Fine wires of a stereotactic machine then guided the electrodes from a fixed point to their target deep in the brain.

The amygdala, Zindel knew, is that portion of the brain most directly related to violence. His ultimate recourse would be sedative surgery, by-passing the amygdala, and destroying a small portion of the hypothalamus. But destroying the limbic system of Gelson was hardly his purpose now, when he could possibly coerce cooperative behavior merely by controlling the left portion of Gelson's brain chemically. The limbic system, as is much of the brain itself, was still a mystery to Zindel as well as other scientists, and he wanted to be careful.

The red light glowed on his console. Zindel leaned to it and spoke directly into an oval screen. "Yes, what is it?"

"Operation Union Bank has been successful, sir. The bomb we planted went off at precisely 5:05 this morning. Several others timed to coincide with the initial blast within a radius of ten city blocks also were effective. There is no report yet as to effect and damage."

Zindel nodded. "Good. Keep in touch. We may go along with the second stage as soon as I have heard from my contact. Are all the other demolition bombs already set in the city area?"

"Yes, sir," the voice said. "We can knock this town down any time you say so."

"Not yet," Zindel said. "I want them to think we are *thinking* it down."

"I don't understand—"

"Don't worry about it, Torchman. We're trying a little elementary psychology here. Over and out."

An hour later, Joe Polo called the Cal Tech earthquake experts to determine if they had traced any seismic activity in the Bay area. Negative, they replied. "All scanners working?" Polo asked. "No chance of a minor quake?"

"Negative," his informant said. "There was a slight disturbance in the Santa Cruz area, 2.9, and another in the San Diego fault amounting to 2.1—but nothing shows around San Francisco."

Polo conveyed his thanks, grinned and lay back for an hour more of shuteye. Then he dressed and went downstairs. He had a quick breakfast in the hotel coffee shop and left before Cantrell could find him.

There were several buildings along his route that looked in bad shape, rubble covering most of the sidewalk, large dents in the walk, and the sides of the buildings blown out. Polo thought this was odd but kept walking until he came to the streets fronting the 20-story Union Bank building near Union Square.

Firemen were extinguishing small fires, and dragging out smouldering wires, chopping them up on the walk. Police cars were spinning their red-lighted turret tops. A voice from the message center kept issuing commands and intercepting signals.

A thickset man, wearing a heavy vest flak shield, came out of the building carrying a small metal box. He walked swiftly to the area outside the police perimeter and deposited the box in a container of oil and distilled water.

"Anything special?" Polo said softly.

The demolition expert turned. His face was haggard and grimed with dirt and sweat. "Some goddam nut," he said. "A demolition bomb synchronized with ones on every fifth floor. Set to go off on a radio signal."

"Anybody hurt?" Polo asked.

"Night watchman got it pretty bad. He found one behind the vent in the gent's room on the

84

fifteenth floor. It went off on him just as he got it out."

"Tough," Palo said, and walked away.

He went back to his room and packed the guns and ammo he thought he might need, along with a pair of field glasses, and went out on the street again. Firemen were cleaning up at the corner of Sutter and Powell when he caught a cab and directed the driver to the waterfront.

Polo paid off the cabbie and walked along the wharf until he found the man with the kind of boat he wanted.

"Angel Island?" the skipper said. "Not much doing there no more. City condemned it, you know—a year ago."

"Any idea why?"

The sailor shrugged. "Some poisonous stuff in the air. Got on the trees, bushes, grass—contaminated a lot of people. The city was afraid they would get more lawsuits than they could afford and closed the place up until a team of Army medics could clear up the junk."

Polo lit a cigarette and gazed moodily across the gray water. He couldn't see the island from that point in the early morning fog. "And what did the medics do about it?"

"Not too much. They claimed some poison gas was coming from a crater below the surface. It used to be Coast Guard property, you know, and they thought maybe they left some junk behind nobody knew they had."

Polo nodded agreeably. "Then what happened?"

The man shrugged wide shoulders, his tan face folding easily into thin leathery wrinkles. "Coast Guard denied it. The Army medics said it was poison gas, bacteriological warfare stuff. Another team went in and found the water had a

85

high mercury level. The bigwigs at City Hall panicked, thought it would ruin the restaurant business—everybody coming up here to eat the fish."

Polo flipped his butt in a high arc into the water. "They called it off?"

The man nodded. "They called it quits. I guess now they hope it will go away by itself."

"No other visitors?" Polo said.

The man looked him over carefully. "You look like a man who likes to look for trouble."

Polo nodded. "Sometimes. Supposing we haggle about a fee and get me out there so we can sort of mosey around."

"You want off at the island?"

Joe Polo grinned shaking his head. "That crazy about finding trouble, I am not. This time we just kind of float around. Not too close. I'll tell you when we get near."

The man got into his boat and balanced Polo as he jumped in. "You're not going ashore, then?"

"Not this time, pal. That part comes later. First we gotta do like the Coast Guard, right?"

The man undid the ropes and fired his engines. "What do *they* do?"

"They make sure the coast is clear."

10

THE POWERFUL LAUNCH circled the island at a respectable distance. Joe Polo screwed up his field glasses and studied the terrain carefully. The skipper leaned back easily controlling his craft, keeping strictly to the periphery Polo had demanded on this first run. They were taking a wide circle approximately a half mile around the area, and at that distance Polo could make out the old Coast Guard buildings on the south end, ringed by surrounding hills. There was no visible movement he could detect. Apart from the sea gulls, neither man nor beast was stirring on Angel Island.

"How long has it been this quiet, pal?" Polo

asked as he surveyed the island.

The skipper shrugged, brown hand tight on the wheel. "It depends on what you mean quiet. Depends also on time of day. You ask Mario—that's me—something funny's been going on for past few months."

"Yeah? Like what?"

"Nighttime is different. Must be something going on. Some working inside. Maybe underneath."

"Underneath? What the hell's underneath? It's an island, isn't it?"

"I do a lotta fishing at night, mister. Sometimes I hear the explosions—and can count all the dead fish I thought I was bringin' back alive."

"Explosions in the water?"

"More like very deep down, you know? Like a volcano is working way down here."

"No volcano in these parts. Got to be something else. Hasn't anybody checked on it?"

Mario nodded. "Oh, yeah. Couple of fellows came over a few weeks ago. I saw their boat floating out to sea later. But I never did see those fellows again."

Polo frowned. "You seem to be telling me somebody is on the island. Like somebody is working the island."

"More like something," the skipper said.

Polo looked at him. "How do you mean?"

Again the swarthy skipper shrugged. "Funny sounds—like animals—screaming moaning sounds. Not human, I'm saying."

"Coming from the island?"

The skipper pointed toward the north cliffs. "That side. Noises of the screaming from that side. Quiet in the middle. At other end—south—I hear the explosions."

"Okay. Now did you ever see anything? Anything at all?" Polo persisted.

The man rubbed his stubbled jaw. "I dunno. Maybe I oughtta not be telling you all this. Maybe it's supposed to be some kind of secret. Government project, maybe?"

Polo shook his head. "No way. They're off the island."

The skipper turned his head nervously. "Well, something funny is going on then. Lotsa times late at night, maybe early morning, I see dumpings on the side of the cliffs."

"Dumpings?"

"Yeah. Like somebody is digging a big hole there."

Polo looked the island over. They had completed the first circular sweep. He signalled the skipper to go around again.

"Closer this time, Mario. But not too close. You think maybe that hole could be a tunnel?"

The skipper stared. "Tunnel to where? Nothing here but Sausalito that side—Tiburon the other. You want to go into San Francisco, you ride your car or take the ferry."

Polo nodded. "Anybody ever wave you off if you got too close?"

Mario shook his head. "No. But one time I could swear somebody triggered something at me. It didn't hit me or the boat, but it cut through the water, just missing us. Lifted the boat a foot in the air. When I got back, guess what I found?"

"You tell me. Your boat was a little charred, maybe?"

The skipper's jaw hung slackly. "How'd you guess that?"

Polo smiled. "Just guessing, that's how."

The skipper lowered his voice near to a whisper. "What it looked like—what it seemed like to me, was a kinda tube of light. Not a torpedo, see? Just this long tube of light that seemed to stretch forever."

Joe Polo snapped his fingers. "Laser."

"Huh?"

"Laser beam, sounds like. Was it on the surface, above or below the water?"

"Under," the skipper said. "Like a long torpedo, only of light. It was quiet, no sound, but it came on fast, like a million miles an hour."

"Then what happened?" Polo said.

The skipper crossed his chest. "I got the hell outta there fast."

It seemed inconceivable to Joe Polo that Zindel could be operating that close to the mainland and the large Bay area cities without being detected. There were other fishermen plying these same waters, the ferry boat running regularly, the sailboats the natives plied in Tiburon Bay and over to Sausalito.

Dumpings, explosions in the water, screaming animal sounds and laser beams seemed too improbable here. In addition to the other hazards of normal traffic in the area, there were the army posts less than fifty miles away with their radar stations, the coast guard and their sonar equipment, the Army Air Force base at Vandenberg, not too far away.

It was all impossible.

Yet somehow Joe Polo thought it could be happening. "Okay, Mario. We go back now. How much would it cost for you to be willing to take me in tonight?"

"A lot."

Guri woke up in a long bare windowless room feeling as if he had been having a bad dream.

His temples throbbed and his brain felt fuzzy. He sat up blinking, wondering where he was. Zindel, he remembered. Something about a man called Sanyo Zindel. Something the man wanted him to do, but he couldn't recall exactly what it was. Had he promised? He couldn't remember.

Then another memory stirred him. This one was a girl. Blonde, shaggy-haired, nice-looking, always smiling—and then the picture changed and she was no longer sweet and smiling but frightened and disturbed, her voice showing it.

"No, Guri, don't," she was saying. "You don't want to do that. Can't you see it's wrong?"

Guri rubbed his head and found it tender and sore, as if he had slept with a confining night cap, something that had pinched his skin. His pulse felt slower than usual and he thought he knew the reason, for that, and then it slipped his mind. Something nagged at him from within that he should be angry about something, something important and that was happening, but he couldn't think of what it was.

He stood up feeling shaken and dizzy. He put his hand again to his head, and then remembered somebody hitting him from behind when he was getting into his car. When was this? he wondered. Yesterday? Last week? Who was it? What had he done?

The door opened suddenly and a man stood there in a white coat. He extended his hand. "Come."

Guri turned and followed the man out and along a dark silent corridor. As he walked, he tried to remember who this man was. He tried to concentrate on that but couldn't. All he remembered was that you were supposed to go with this man in the white coat.

They turned at a bend in the stone corridor and Guri heard a faint humming sound. It set up a peculiar reaction inside him, as if a motor was racing somewhere but he wanted it to be running inside him.

The man in the white coat stopped and opened a door. He beckoned and Guri stepped through and saw the man at the far end of the large light room sitting in a wheelchair.

"He's ready," the man in the white coat said.

"Good. Leave us."

The white-coated man left the room and the door closed silently behind him. Guri stood motionless, only his eyes following. His head felt very heavy and he wanted to sit down or maybe go to sleep again. He wondered if he wasn't hungry and couldn't remember if he had eaten lately.

The man in the wheelchair put his left hand out toward a console running along the wall with a lot of dials, knobs, arrows and scopes. "Well, Guri," he said, "I guess it's time we got to work." Guri nodded, pleased with the sound of the man's voice. "Am I hungry?" he said.

The man stared at him with large yellow eyes. "Do you think you are?"

Guri shrugged, still smiling. "Think? What's that?"

The man in the chair frowned. "No. You are not hungry. Come over here, please."

Guri stepped toward the man.

"Do you remember what we spoke about yesterday?"

Guri shook his head smiling. "Remember? What's that?"

The man tapped the arm of his wheelchair. Was

Gelson faking? he wondered. Had they given him too much of the tranquillity pattern? "What is your name?" he said suddenly.

Guri stood smiling, ears pleased at the man's voice. He looked down at the man's body and wondered why it was sitting that way in the chair with the large wheels.

The man muttered something angrily under his breath. "Your name is Guri. Do you remember that?"

Guri rubbed his head. "This hurts. Am I hungry?"

The man in the chair eyed him steadily. "Your stomach tells you if you are hungry. Do you remember where that is?"

Guri smiled and turned toward the door. "Thank you," he said, and began walking away toward the door.

Zindel blew his cheeks out. "Wait! Come back!" he said. He swore when Gelson kept walking, then spun his wheels quickly toward the console and touched a button.

Gelson stopped one foot in the air. The foot came back slowly to the floor and he stood there facing the door.

Zindel pressed the button on his console again. "Come here, Guri," he ordered.

Guri turned and saw the man in the chair again. He thought he looked familiar. He took a step toward him to say hello or something, but his legs gave way under him and he fell to the floor. He noticed there were metal edges on the floor forming a grid pattern. Something stirred in his memory.

"Get up, Guri," the man said.

Guri looked at the man and then at the floor. Then he looked beyond the man at the long black console with the many lights, dials, and knobs. He frowned. There was something there he did not like but he couldn't remember what it was. He stared at the console.

There was a faint humming sound. Zindel turned his head and saw a thin wisp of smoke coming from the console. He held his hand up. "Stop, Gelson," he ordered. "Don't do that!"

Guri kept frowning at the long panel board, not hearing the man. Zindel came back to the panel board and saw the red needles spinning. He banged the board where some light kept going off and on. He pressed a button marked *EMERGENCY RELEASE*.

"Don't do that," Guri said, and Zindel's hand hung in mid-air.

Zindel turned his head. "Don't do what?"

Gelson's lips moved silently. Veins throbbed in his head. He took a deep breath, then exhaled. He shook his head, his eyes worried. "I—I forget."

Zindel spun his chair around to face the young psychic. "You had power once, do you remember?"

Gelson frowned. "Power? What is power?"

"You could think about something. Make it happen by projecting energy. Do you remember that?"

Gelson rubbed his forehead. "Something is not clear here. There is interference."

Zindel nodded. He was pleased that the experiment had worked with Gelson, proving that his powerful mind could be reached and affected by his methods. They had gone too far with it, over-corrected to some degree, but he thought this was to be expected, and no real harm done. Now that they knew how to reach him, they could withdraw the pressure by degrees until he was amenable to suggestion and still able to focus on his own amazing energy. There was still time to experiment, Zindel knew, and with a prize like Gelson too much at stake to blunder and ruin everything by forceful measures.

Zindel smiled at Gelson. Better to go one step at a time. He was like a child now, and so he would treat him as one. "Do you want to see the girl again, Guri? You want Rita?"

Gelson frowned. It was a familiar sound. "Rita?"

Zindel's eyes blazed. Incredible that the amygdaloid nucleus could actually control so much of Gelson's emotional range. He smiled warmly again. "You will see her. I will have her brought to your room. Would you like that?"

Gelson thought about it. Frowning he said, "I— I don't know—"

Zindel pressed his red lever and called into the set. "Come in, Otto. Gelson is going back to his room."

A moment later, the white-coated attendant entered. He nodded at Zindel and walked toward Gelson who stared at him unblinkingly.

"We go the other way now, Otto. He is overstimulated, but while compliant, is like a vegetable. Look at him."

Otto looked, nodded, and shrugged. "They all get that way, don't they?"

Zindel hit the arm of his chair. "Not this one. Reverse procedure now and reactivate the hypothalamus. I want him to be useful to us. I want him ready to work by tomorrow."

Otto nodded. "Come along, you," he said to Gelson.

Guri followed him out the door smiling.

... 11

THE LANDING AT MIDNIGHT was too tricky. The full moon obscured by thick drifting clouds provided good cover, but the beach landing area was treacherously lined with jagged rocks. Joe Polo at last gave up any idea of bringing the launch onto the sandy area under the high bluffs of the island north shore.

He had Mario cut the engines and they let the tide swing the powerful cruiser in toward a shadowy inlet. But again the sharp rocks jutting just above the water surface were enough to send them off and around again.

They were going around for the third time, circling in a tightening ring when it happened.

There was a loud humming sound coming from deep beneath the water. Polo signalled to the skipper to cut his engines in order for them to discover the source for this strange effect. There was a loud hiss from the port side, accompanied by a great wave which broke over the boat.

Mario turned, shielding his eyes from the spray and his voice was filled with fear as he yelled: "Look out! There's some kind of sea monster!"

Polo was shaking his head, cursing himself for having hired a superstitious fisherman, when he saw the huge gray shape looming directly off their bow. It towered twenty feet above them, like some giant reptilian relic of the past, and as Polo stared incredulous at the sight, he heard a clanking noise and giant jaws opened wide, ready to devour them.

"Start your engine! Reverse!" he yelled at the staring Mario, pale under the moon's fleeting light. Polo saw he was paralyzed with fear and struck him across the face. "Move, man! That thing's not real! It's a mechanical mousetrap—can't you see?"

The towering jaws were wet with the water's spill, seemingly some crazy drooling monster of the deep, a vast steel-headed juggernaut of the bay. Mario recoiled, crossing himself, unable to move. Polo had to do it for him, reaching across to fire the port engine, and as it caught, desperately threw the lever into reverse.

The tide was strong and they drifted closer to the great dripping jaws, unable to skirt free. At the last moment, Polo cursed again and grabbed Mario. "Jump! Get out of here! Let the boat go, Mario—I'll buy you another—"

But the frightened fisherman only stared with wide-eyed wonder, frozen with fright. Polo hit him again then, to knock him over the side, and dived himself. As he hit the water, he heard the grinding crunch and saw the powerboat tilted on its stern in the open jaws of the mechanical monster. The jaws slowly ground together and the boat disappeared into the slimy maw, splintering. The monster sank slowly taking it below the surface. The water foamed and Polo swam for his life.

Polo looked for Mario but the fog was rolling in now and he saw nothing but the fuzzy yellow patches. He yelled and struck out for the rocky inlet they had passed earlier. When he reached it, he paused again, waiting for the fisherman. But he saw and heard nothing. There were too many points now where Mario might have swum ashore. Polo shook the water from his eyes, and pulled himself past the last rock guarding the shore.

He cursed himself for being careless, wasting Mario's boat, and perhaps his life. Zindel undoubtedly had sonar and radar working for him and had picked up the sounds of the cruiser. The mechanical shark was something right out of Jules Verne; but worked, he had to admit. A moment more and he and Mario would have been imprisoned inside those steel jaws, and dragged below the surface for the improbable meeting with the renegade mad scientist Zindel.

Polo climbed up the high slope of the overhanging cliff, digging his heels into the moist sand, scattering rock and gravel as he fought his way to the top. His hands were at the crest now, reaching for a hold on the tufts of grass rimming the cliff when he heard the frightening sound of baying hounds.

He pulled himself to chin level and stared into

the night. He saw the huge dark shapes thrusting toward him, yellow eyes blazing in the darkness, heading straight for him. He had his guns and could have picked them off, but then he would definitely have revealed his presence. Instead he silently cursed and let himself drop again down the slope to the water and its guarding sentinel rocks.

When he reached the bottom and was edging around the cliff side, he heard the sound of sliding rocks. Polo flattened himself against the cliff wall and when the shadowy figure came at him from his left, he was ready with his knife. He plunged it deep into the man's gut with an upward ripping force, killing him instantly. The man fell back and dropped the rifle he held. Polo pushed him into the water, and picked up the piece. It was a .32 carbine, good army weapon for hunting; and Polo had the odd feeling now that he was the hunter tonight, as well as the prey.

There was the crunch of gravel above and he looked up in time to see a man hurtling down at him, head first, arms outstretched.

"Jesus, what gives?" Polo said, and stepping aside, he clubbed the falling target squarely over the skull, quickly reversed the weapon and rammed it into the fallen man's belly, lifted it again and smashed his cheekbone. The man fell back into the water with a gurgling sound and Polo, who had seen other men die, turned away to improve his vulnerable position.

The man who had come to him from his left seemed to have gotten there suddenly, and Polo slipped back into the water and slowly swam around the corner of the cliff. There was a dark opening there, a cave, and he wondered how many others were in there waiting, or were already on their way out to get him.

He swam back to the spot where the water monster had come rearing up at them, ducked below and swam down for twenty feet. There was a bright light below, so he surfaced and kept swimming.

Polo had now established that Zindel, or whoever was inhabiting the island, had an underwater grotto operating; a cave that conceivably led to the main works, while the upper cliff topside provided access to another section of the island empire.

He remembered the abandoned fort and Coast Guard buildings at the far side of the island. There could be cover there, he thought, places where he would be less exposed; and perhaps he might be able to hide there until he had found out if Gelson really was a prisoner on the island.

Without the boat, he wondered briefly how he would get Gelson out if he did find him, but there would be time enough to worry about that. The great rescue seemed far ahead into the future and his survival this night was the key move.

He reached a wooded area which offered cover and crept ashore when the moon was again briefly covered by clouds. The fog had been lifting gradually as the night wind picked up and Polo shivered, soaked to the bone, and struck out at a run for the standing grove of pines, his leg injury forgotten.

Working his way around, drifting in the shadows like an Indian, he kept himself warm and alive at the same time. He was close to the old walls of the abandoned fort when he heard the loud rumbling noises beneath his feet. He had already seen the visible evidence of Zindel's scientific mind at work, and moved carefully, head down, searching for the source of the volcano-like activity below the surface of the earth.

He marked its center and moved off, waiting in the shadows of the old fort, rubbing himself, beating his hands against his wet clothing and cold skin.

Polo wasn't the least bit surprised when a portion of the earth rumbled loudly again, and then slid back, hinging like a shelf for a rising elevator. He was close enough now to see the man coming up on the steel shaft. He was wearing a dark hood over a night hunting suit, carrying a long rifle. He stepped off the shaft carefully, and was lighting a cigarette when Polo clubbed him from behind. The man groaned softly and Polo killed him.

It was easier taking off the man's warm and dry outfit than his own wet one, but he made his fingers move fast. He drew the man's body aside into the shadows of the fort and threw it under some rubble.

He waited until the lift was about to lower and pulling the hood over his face, he stepped on the platform and allowed it to take him slowly down into the underground grotto.

Rita Quimby looked searchingly into Gelson's face. He was sitting quietly at a small desk tapping its surface with the handle of a small spoon. Other objects lay on the desk. A key, a nail, and a ring.

"What's happening?" she whispered.

Guri shrugged. "I must've blacked out. I lost track of things. When I was waking up, I had a kind of weird dream. Like I was being on a table down here and somebody was operating on me." He fingered his scalp gently. "My head hurts."

"Let me look at it," she said. She came over and parted his hair. There were small red marks close to the rim of his forehead, a small shaven patch on the left side of his head. She touched it with the tips of her fingers. "Does this hurt?"

He winced, drawing away. "Yeah, like it burns."

"Well, it looks to me as if they did an EEG on you. Can you remember anything at all?"

His brow knitted and he sighed and nodded. "You're right. It wasn't any dream. But there was a time when I thought I died. There wasn't anything to me at all, no power, no will. I couldn't think. Really bombed outta my skull."

She nodded, thumbing to the closed door behind her. "Maybe they're hearing everything we're saying. Have you seen Dr. Zindel again?"

Gelson nodded. "Now I remember that. Only I don't know what happened. I know the other time, he caught me with some kind of electric dragout on that grid floor of his lab. A current came out of it and grabbed me. I couldn't move and it shocked me out of my wits. I don't remember much after that until the first time I woke up and somebody was making me drink something."

Rita shrugged. "They've been preparing you for something. No question about it. I hope you realize what's going on here now. This isn't any goodwill scientific clinic, you know."

"I know," Gelson said. "They gave me these things I used to do things with. To sort of practice again, get my energy up."

She looked down, puzzled. "How do you do that?"

Guri smiled. "I guess you never caught my act. Saw me do my tricks."

She shook her head. "I've heard of you, of course."

He picked up the spoon with the tips of his fingers. "Here is how it all started. Watch." He rubbed the end of the spoon lightly with his thumb. To the girl's amazement, the spoon began to curl. "I don't have to use the magic words," he said.

The spoon kept curling until it had formed almost a loop. Guri gave it to her. "You'll notice it isn't warm. I didn't rub it, use friction of any kind."

"But how—?"

He shrugged. "Spoons are always easy. Now watch the key." He picked up the key in one hand, ran the other lightly over it. Almost instantly, it began to bend, and kept bending until it was almost at a right angle.

"Remind me not to lend you my car keys," she said.

"Well, anyway, it's coming back. I'm not even thinking too hard about this stuff now. That's like my normal way. Now with the elevator that day we met in your building, I really had to concentrate—think hard about getting the elevator door to close, and go down. Mostly because I broke some metal part of it when I came up. So nobody could follow me."

She looked worried. "No wonder Zindel wants you to work for him!"

Guri smiled. "But he wants me to do things I don't think I can do. How am I gonna pull a plane down outta the sky?"

She made her eyes widen. "He wants you to do that?"

Guri nodded. "Well, yeah—that's one of them."

"But, why?"

103

He shrugged. "Beats me. To show somebody what he—what we can do, I guess. It's about the same stuff that guy Adams of the State Department was talking to me about. To be some kind of secret weapon with this energy talent I got. Only with Adams, he thought it would be okay because it would be for my own government, see? Only I can't see that it makes any difference. Why can't they ask me to do good stuff, something that would help people?"

"Can you do that?"

"I don't know," Gelson said. "But, maybe. You know, if somebody had a tumor or some disease, maybe I could pull it outta him, or maybe heal it with a bolt of my energy—like it could be a laser beam."

"But you don't know if you can do that, Guri," she said. "Maybe it stops right here, with the spoons and the key and—" Then she remembered the trick with the elevator and the filing cabinets and the tapes. "Sorry, I just remembered what you did to our files. Also, you did direct me to your apartment mentally, didn't you?"

"Yeah. If I knew where we were now, maybe I could direct somebody to come after us and get us out."

"I think I know where we are," she said.

Gelson stared. "How would you know?"

"Somebody left a newspaper in my room, accidentally. It was the *San Francisco Ledger*."

"You mean we're in San Francisco?"

"Maybe not, not in the city. But we're close. I can smell the water. We saw the water from Zindel's window through the tunnel, remember. And anyway, it doesn't have to be exactly where we think it is for it to work."

"Why not?" he asked.

"Because all you have to do is start broadcasting your energy power mentally," she said. "The State Department and the Army Air Force will be using radar and sonar to pick us up."

Guri smiled. "Hey, you're right. I'm gonna start—"

The smile faded from his lips as the door opened. The giant Felix stood there a moment, then advanced slowly, his huge hands hanging down, his thick lips drooling, his eyes blazing in their madman's light.

"HERE'S YOUR CHANCE," Rita whispered. "Stop him."

"How?" Guri said. "There's nothing metal on him."

"Mentally, I mean. Turn him around. Make him go back."

Guri looked at the advancing giant. "Right on. I'll give him an A-blast right between the eyes." He took a quick breath, and tried to make his thoughts enter the shambling man's brain. "Go back," he said under his breath. "Go back."

Felix lumbered closer toward them, his dull yellow teeth showing in his idiot grin.

Guri stood his ground until the huge servant

was only a few steps away. "Back, back!" he said, trying to force the thought between them. "Turn around, creep!"

At the last instant, the giant stopped, shook his head as if puzzled, then took another step forward, his big hairy hand stretched out toward Rita.

"I can't stop him," Guri said, sweating. "I don't think he's got a brain to reach."

"Forget his brain, then," she said quickly. "Aim lower—at his mechanism—maybe his heart."

"That's a thought," Gelson said. He frowned, drew his head down, and centered his thought at the huge barrel chest of the man.

Felix stopped. He blinked. His outstretched hand wavered and then came down to his side.

"You did it!" Rita said smiling. "Make him lie down."

"Yeah," Gelson said. "Down, Felix. Down, boy!"

The giant looked at them, shaking his shaggy head, as Gelson centered every ounce of his strength in the thought, aiming directly at the chest.

Felix made a sad whimpering sound.

Down, down. All the way down, Gelson willed.

Felix sagged at the knees. Then like a huge tree falling, he toppled headfirst to the floor and lay there quietly.

Rita clapped her hands. "Terrific! Remember how you did that."

Gelson wiped the sweat beading his brow. "Okay, now what?"

She took his hand. "Let's take a walk. Maybe we can find our way out of this place."

"Say, that's right," Gelson said. "Why didn't I think of that."

They went through the door and stopped. Otto was waiting for them wearing his white coat, holding a gun. "Dr. Zindel thought this might happen," he said. "Come along, you two."

The hinged earth-surfaced lid folded back into place as Joe Polo stepped on the vertical shaft. Twin steel pulleys ran along the side down to the lower level, and Polo picked one and pulled. There was the low rumbling sound of a counterweight mechanism below, and the flat ledge he was on descended.

The lift went down slowly on a central shaft in a circular vault, the rock-hewn sides of a subterranean grotto. From his descending height, Polo hoped to see the labrynth of Zindel's underground factory, but was disappointed. Far below, perhaps sixty feet, he could see a sentry at the bottom sitting at a small desk facing a small TV monitoring screen. As he drew closer, Polo was able to see flickering gray images on the screen, a lot of snow and scrambled abstract pictures.

There were three landings along the way extending into hallways, but Polo figured he might be hopelessly lost or picked up at the outside points, and stayed with the lift. As it neared the bottom, he was ready to jump the sentry, but the man stayed sitting, his back to Polo, merely asking over his shoulder, "How'd it go?"

Polo stepped off onto solid stone, tensely awaiting the next move. "Nothing to see. Foggy out," he muttered. The sentry nodded absently and kept his eyes on the set. Polo kept walking, turned left at the bend in the corridor. He came to a small cell-like room and looked through the open door. A giant of a man lay on the floor, near

108

a desk. On the desk, Polo saw a bent spoon, a twisted key, a ring, and a nail.

The hood over his face, part of the costume he had inherited from the sentry outside, bothered Polo's vision and breathing. He threw it off and looked closely at the metal items. They were still warm to his touch and he wondered where Guri Gelson was at the moment.

He heard a rustling movement behind him and turned too late. A heavy arm came around his throat pressing hard on his jugular and he was yanked back on his heels. Polo swung back with his right arm but he was held as easily as a baby by someone with superhuman strength.

As his heels left the floor and he was lifted high in the air, Polo managed to turn and see the ugly sadistic face of the giant who had been face down on the floor. He punched at it and saw blood spatter the man's face, blossoming like some red flower. The giant roared and swung him higher with both arms. Polo twisted but could not reach him now, and the massive misshapen figure holding him aloft swung him back easily over his head and threw him against the stone wall.

Polo crashed into unconsciousness, his head making an ugly crunching sound, and slid to the floor. The giant stood over him, wiping the blood off his face with the back of his hand. He stood over the prostrate form of Polo growling, and pawed at his limp body. Gutteral animal sounds came from his throat, but Polo heard none of them.

The giant reached down then, picked up Polo as if he were a sack of flour, and threw him over his shoulder. Then he walked off with his prisoner, turning right under a low stone arch, and went down a winding stone stairway. The air was damp here, the flooring large, irregular paving stones. Near the stairway was a thick nail-studded door, with an open-barred slot at the top.

As the giant opened the door, a gaunt animal tethered to a stake growled menacingly. The giant laughed and threw the body of Joe Polo down on the cold stones.

He waved his hands to the beast. It growled and tried to reach Polo, straining at its leash. The giant kneeled and stretched his hand out to untie the rope.

Joe Polo stirred. His eyes opened and he took in the dungeon-like surroundings at a glance. He opened his clenched hand and saw a thick nail there, the spike Gelson had left. The giant's back was toward him as he fumbled with the knots binding the beast. Polo sucked in air quickly, rolled silently to his knees, and then with his heels tucked beneath him, catapulted toward the massive towheaded man.

The spike in his hand struck home savagely, and the giant stiffened as the nail was imbedded in the back of his neck. He opened his mouth to roar his pain, could only gasp helplessly. He slumped slowly to the straw-littered stones, paralyzed now from the nerve-severing blow, and dying fast. The huge beast growled once more and pulled hard against the loosening knot.

"He's all yours, baby. Eat," Polo said, and walked away, closing the dungeon door carefully behind him.

Guri Gelson and Rita Quimby sat nervously in the small anteroom where Zindel's assistant Otto had placed them. "I guess you couldn't do anything with that man, could you?" she said.

Gelson lifted his shoulders and his hands apologetically. "When somebody is pointing a gun at your belly, it's awful hard to concentrate on something else."

"What do you think will happen now?"

"I think Otto is some kind of doctor here, helping Zindel. Maybe doing neurosurgery, like what they were trying to do with me. His real name is Otto Compor."

"How do you know that?"

"It just came to me. It was all in the memory file in your building. All that stuff on tape. Sometimes when I erase it just by being close, all the stuff sort of flows into me—like I get the feedback in my brain without reading or listening." He lifted his shoulders again, defensively. "Another of my little tricks. I don't know how that works, either."

"It doesn't matter. You're no freak. You must have been given this gift, all of them, for some purpose. Some day it will all happen. I'm sure. You'll do something very important for the world."

"Right now, I'd settle for doing something important for you and me. I don't trust that guy Zindel. Anybody who claims Oppenheimer stole his theory paper has to be some kind of nut."

Rita gestured futilely. "But what's he trying to do? Take over the world? Can he be serious?"

Gelson thought about it. "I don't think it's that so much," he said slowly. "He probably wants some kind of international recognition and to get that he has to show he has power. Look how the Arab nations got the world to knuckle under just by holding the monopoly on oil. Well, Zindel can do the same thing in another way."

"What way is that?"

"I guess by destroying their power. Without power, electricity, any big city can't function—any government would have to come to terms. And maybe Zindel knows how to use what I've got to get what he wants."

"But how, Guri? You can't stop all the elevators in the world, can you?"

He looked at her gloomily. "Maybe not, but I can probably stop TV broadcasts all over, change radar waves, disorganize a lot of things they take for granted. Like I said, I don't know yet all the things I can do. But Zindel probably has it all figured out. Maybe he'll use me like some kind of intercontinental laser missile, my brain wave energy reinforced somehow by some current he has, and then—*blam!* Everybody goes into instant whammo!"

"I don't believe it," Rita said. "If you just get going on broadcasting some kind of bleep signal now, the Air Force will home in on your signal and rescue us."

"I would strongly advise against your attempting that," a cold voice said. They jumped nervously and the door opened. Zindel sat hunched in his wheelchair. His talon-like hand lifted and beckoned. "Come along, Miss Quimby. I want to show you and Mr. Gelson something that might appreciably influence your judgment."

They followed him a short distance down the corridor. He faced a wall and something glowed in his hand and sent out a faint signal. The wall slid back. Zindel motioned them forward. "It's only an elevator," he said. "We have to go down a few stories to see these exhibits."

Once inside, the door closed behind them. Gelson cocked his head, as if straining to hear the mechanism running the quietly moving car. He heard nothing other than his own accelerated breathing. He frowned, uncertain as to whether he could halt this moving car or not. Better leave it alone for now, he told himself. Maybe save it for later in case you really need some kind of miracle.

The door swished open again in seconds and Zindel gestured for them to follow. As they stepped out, he flashed his hand-held beam and the door closed.

"This way," Zindel said. His wheels turned and his wheelchair moved silently ahead. The corridor was long and narrow, lit by overhead lights. They passed a series of doors, with cut-out slits at the top, some barred, others with glass panels. When Zindel stopped, they faced a dark glass extending from ceiling to the floor.

"You were speaking of experiments before," Zindel said. At their confused reaction, he smiled thinly. "Naturally every word here that is said is taped and can be heard in my quarters. Be that as it may, you also spoke of purpose—what purpose I could possibly have? Am I a madman out to conquer the world? To gain power? Wealth? Recognition?"

Zindel's voice became coldly arrogant. "Would you believe all of them? Yes, my dears, it is quite true, and incredibly well within my reach. Without Mr. Gelson here, it might have taken longer, but assuredly it was always part of my plan.

"But with him and his tantric energy to assist me, there can be no question at all now. That which I desire will come to pass. Now as to pressure, the ultimate commitment—please gaze into the glass. You will see some rather interesting examples—perhaps shocking to you—of our recent experiments in brain alteration methods."

As the interior became clearly seen, he added, "This is a one-way glass. You cannot be seen by the patients."

They looked and Rita gasped and turned her head away. Shambling human wrecks without life in their eyes, robot-like stiff forms that once were human, all lustreless now as if they were vegetables. They sat or leaned against the wall, or stood staring at the wall, at nothing; acting like figures, designs in a frieze. There were women and men, but there was nothing lifelike among any of them. They were a torpid, vapid wasteland.

"How cruel!" Rita said. "What gave you the right?"

Zindel shrugged. "Unfortunately, what you see before you are the failures. But we always have hopes, and are always ready to try new techniques. Now with you, Miss Quimby, I give you my word we will be very careful when we study your brain. We wouldn't want anything amiss to happen to it."

She stared speechless, eyes dilated in fright.

"That's the pressure point, my dear. How can Mr. Gelson refuse to cooperate with me now, knowing you are the next subject, the hostage completely dependent upon his good work? Do you agree, Mr. Gelson?"

Gelson stared into Zindel's face.

... 13

THE INSTRUMENT BOARD on the huge black console lit up and various scopes began ticking. Zindel nodded, pleased.

"Splendid, Mr. Gelson. We are picking up your thought waves in increased energy output. As you can see, all I need do is observe the needle move and know whether or not you're trying."

Gelson pushed back the lock of hair from his perspiring forehead. "It's not what you think, Dr. Zindel. I mean, it doesn't work the way you think it does, the way you want it to. Sometimes I get results by concentrating. But there are plenty of other times when nothing happens. Nothing at all. And then, there are times, when

I can leave the room seemingly without anything happening, and then all of a sudden things do happen. What I'm trying to tell you is, I can't always control it."

Zindel smiled, hands folded across his thin chest. "You will learn how, my boy. That's what I'm here for. To help you. Once you learn how to harness your power, we can move the universe."

Guri looked unconvinced. "Like how?"

Zindel propelled his chair to a low table. A wine glass rested on it and Zindel picked it up. He held it outstretched between his thin fingers for Guri to see. "We'll start with this, Gelson. As you know, a thin glass can be shattered by higher vibrations. We will gear you up to it as we do in ordinary biofeedback. First, I ask you to look directly at the glass in my hand."

Guri shrugged, with a sidelong glance at Rita Quimby. "Okay, I'm looking at the glass in your hand."

"Fine. Now concentrate. Will it to break."

Gelson stared hard at the glass. It held its form but the magnetometer on the console began to tick erratically. "Higher," Zindel commanded. "You're not on target. You're thinking of my hand. Perhaps hoping the glass shatters and cuts it. No, Gelson, think of the glass. Only of the glass."

Gelson leaned forward. His veins throbbed and bulged on his forehead. He frowned, willing the glass to destruction. *Come on,* he thought mentally holding it, *break already, god-dammit!* His eyes fixed rigidly on the glass as if he were boring a hole through it. Suddenly there was a popping sound, a tingling explosion, the shattering sound of glass breaking.

Zindel opened his hand. There was nothing in it but the stem. "Marvelous," he said. "Now you're learning how to do it."

Guri moved toward the wheelchair and table looking down at the glass particles littering the floor. He shook his head in wonder. "You know, that's the first time I ever did glass. Metal and things like that, I could always do." He glanced back at Rita smiling happily. "First time I did glass. Did you notice?"

She smiled wryly. "Marvelous. That leaves wood, paper, and stone for you to get into next."

Guri flushed. "Well, you know, I had to try it, didn't I?" He shook his head disturbed, and turned to Zindel. "Okay, I did it, but it really was very hard work. I mean, I had to use every last bit of energy in me to break that little glass. So, what I'm trying to say is, that little wine glass is a long way from bringing a plane down outta the sky, or otherwise moving the universe, like you say."

Zindel nodded. "I understand, but for every major breakthrough, there has to be a minor start, a beginning. Well, now you have done it, and know you have, and can repeat it if it ever becomes necessary. You managed to focus your entire energy force at an object, and then raise the level—it went above 2,000 megacycles, by the way—and at its highest point, the glass broke. But your energy force was going much higher at the time. Had your concentration not been broken, you could have easily broken that heavy plate glass window there, with a view to my gardens and the tunnel to the bay."

Gelson shook his head. "Hey, come on. Be reasonable. That glass has gotta be an inch thick. You couldn't break it even throwing a hard baseball at it."

Zindel shrugged. "We'll let it go for the mo-

117

ment. We're below the water level and I wouldn't care for us to be inundated by several million tons of water. But there is something else now you can try."

Guri hesitated, putting his hand to his forehead. "Hey, but gee—I get a headache doing this stuff, you know."

"Unfortunate," Zindel said. "But you would feel much worse knowing that Miss Quimby was undergoing psychosurgery, wouldn't you?"

"Yeah. No doubt about it. Okay, what's next? Maybe I can do it—for the laughs."

"Let's find out something else about your amazing power," Zindel said. He waved his hand to the particles of shattered glass on the floor. "I understand you are also able to teleport objects, at times. Now here is the mess of glass on the floor near my wheelchair. Ordinarily, we would clean it up with a broom and dustpan. Rather archaic means in these advanced days of science, wouldn't you agree?"

Gelson shrugged. "Well, yeah, maybe—but—"

Zindel pointed at the glass on the floor. "Make it go away, Gelson. Blast it off, melt it down, or just make it disappear—any way you like. I'll give you five minutes."

Gelson remembered other times when he actually had moved objects from one room into another. Strange outlandish happenings he was afraid to discuss with people. A teapot suddenly rising off the kitchen table, going into the cupboard. An ash tray moving off the table to another at the far end of the room. Then there was the time when he was certain he had actually teleported himself, thought he had flown through the air, and somehow magically or mysteriously arrived at a building where he had an appointment. But he was

118

never certain, and finally decided he had taken a cab and forgotten the incident.

But he had read about teleporting, the moving of material objects. It fascinated him because of the possibilities. As for making things disappear, that was downright impossible, he thought, because then you were disrupting molecules and their structure. Nobody human could do that.

And yet he knew he already had.

During his wartime service, he had been so concerned about all the tapes he had somehow fouled up by his presence, that at the last, he willed the remaining spool to disappear. Go on, get lost, get the hell out, he mentally commanded it. And seconds later, he opened his eyes, and it was gone. No trace of it in the files, nothing in the room or anywhere, and he never did locate it again.

That was his best, he thought. But *now* what? he wondered. Like, what was he going to do for an encore?

"We're waiting," Zindel said.

Guri closed his eyes. Okay, you cosmic powers out there, he prayed silently. Let's see it for the West Coast. Let's clean up all that broken glass on the man's floor.

He visualized how nice it would be, how incredulous Zindel would look, how Rita would stare shaking her head, saying this was really too much. He heard her gasp, then Zindel drew his breath in sharply.

"Well," Zindel said. "Now that is really remarkable!"

He opened his eyes then and saw nothing at all on the floor near the wheelchair, not a sparkling speck, no glitter of any kind, no debris moved into the corner or under Zindel's feet.

The glass was gone!

Guri stared down at the floor, feeling his heart thump. *Well, hey—that is really a trick, you know?* And silently he said his thanks to the powers out there in space who had made this possible.

No kidding, guys, thanks a lot, he breathed. *It sure as hell beats bending spoons and keys and fixing clocks and watches.* He looked at Rita. Her eyes were wide with disbelief still fixed on the floor. Then they moved to roll to the four corners of the room, still showing disbelief, and then they came back to him, and they were the eyes of a little girl who had just seen her first big magic trick.

"Don't tell me," she said. "You don't know how you did it."

Meanwhile Joe Polo was snaking down long hallways, ducking in and out of recesses in the walls, keeping a wary eye on the various sentries Zindel had stationed around his operation. It was a game of hare and hounds, and Polo knew it well. But he still sweated, nerveless though he was. The big tricks were still ahead of him. Finding Zindel, then Gelson and the girl.

Wrecking the operation then, and getting them out.

Alive would be better, he told himself. He didn't want to leave too many dead bodies around in the halls to alert the whole damn place. Better to be careful and step out of the way. He was too old in the game to be trigger-happy.

Another bend in the corridor, and Polo stopped, feeling a chill run down his spine. His hackles rose and he shook his head, wondering if he really had seen what he thought. He came back to the large wall-size glass for another look.

There were the shapes and bodies, ostensibly human, but behaving as if in a dream or catatonic state. Men and women with no expression on their faces, no light in their eyes, unsmiling, moving with effort, fixed in odd positions when they rested, staring out into nothingness like vegetables.

Like zombies, Polo thought. Were they clonings, Zindel's repetitions of humans, or the result of some bizarre technique being carried on here in the name of science?

He heard footsteps and flattened himself against the wall. A stocky middle-aged man walked by wearing a white coat and an air of authority. He was alone and Polo put an arm around his neck as he passed and let him feel the blade of his long knife at the side of his throat. "Your name, please?" Polo said into his ear. "We don't want to kill the wrong people."

The man's eyes rolled behind heavy glasses. "Otto—Dr. Otto Compor—"

Polo pressed the blade closer nicking the skin. "What's your trick here, Doctor?"

The man cringed feeling the blade nick his skin. His voice was strangled, gutteral. "This—this work—neurosurgery. I work for Dr. Zindel. Please—"

Polo turned him around. "Let's go into your office, Doc."

Compor fiddled with the knob and Polo stepped close beside him. The door swung open, and Polo went in with him, locking his arm as if they were buddies taking the tour together.

"In here," Otto said.

The office was small, the desk littered with papers. Tests and forms. Photographs. Research items. There was a large glass in the wall. Behind it gray forms moved slowly.

"Mirror on the other side?" Polo asked.

Compor nodded, perspiring, his jowls shaking. "Yes, the one-way mirror for observation."

Polo indicated the patients on the other side. "Where'd you get the material, Doc? Volunteers?"

Compor paled. "We pick them up. Derelicts, mostly. Down and outers, on Skid Row. The bums, drunks, hippies, prostitutes—they have no future. We thought perhaps we could find out what made them that way—"

"It's not that complicated," Polo said. "Usually it's a little something called life. Or getting kicked in the ass by Fate. Or Lady Luck spitting in your eye. In other words, it happens, Doc, or didn't you know?"

Otto Compor shook his head. He saw no mercy in his visitor's blazing eyes. "You do not understand. It was my field, yes—but Dr. Zindel asked me to work for him. He promised there would be enough experiments for me to prove my theories —in time, it would be of benefit to the race. What you see here is nothing. There are always failures. We don't know enough yet. The brain is too sensitive, too tricky—we think we have it and then it slips through our fingers."

"Nothing to it," Polo said. "You drill a little hole in the skull, cut out what you think they don't need—left side, right side—but somehow you never get the parts all put together, do you, Doc?"

"The treatment started with curing violent epileptics," Compor said. "First anti-convulsant drugs, then the destruction of specific cells in the patients' amygdala—a part of the limbic system. Zindel wanted us to move faster. To kill the cells

122

with a proton beam, without surgery. The tissues are not damaged, and you can remove a cancerous pituitary that way, without surgery, you understand. But too much stimulation and they cannot be tranquillized any more. They are unpredictable now, will fly into a rage if anything disturbs them, tear a teddy bear or a dog to pieces. Any loud sound will set them off. That is why it is so quiet here, you notice."

"I thought the walls were soundproofed," Polo said.

Otto went to the door. "No, listen," he said, opening it.

Polo stepped toward the opening. He heard nothing but the breathing of the patients. He nodded, whispering, "You're right, Doc. Can't hear a thing."

Then he suddenly pushed Dr. Otto Compor across the room into the midst of the moving patients. Before the man could recover, Polo picked up a clipboard and banged it loudly against the door. "Now hear this," he yelled. "This is the sound you've been waiting for. Battle stations, everybody."

He stepped back and shut the door quickly. Through the dark glass, he could see them moving in on Dr. Compor, their faces working now with strange grimaces. They were hitting him and knocking him down and doing a lot of terrible things to him, when Polo thought he had seen enough, and walked out and down the corridor.

...14

SANYO ZINDEL RUBBED HIS hands together. "Well, now that you have some confidence, Gelson, let us move ahead. Please keep in mind the terrible things we have in store for Miss Quimby. Think about how guilty you would feel if you permitted us to experiment on her in our psychosurgery ward—and then you will feel obliged to do as I ask."

Guri stroked his throat. He glanced at Rita and saw her standing pale and frightened, and knew there was to be no more evasion. "Okay, name it," he said. "I'll see what I can do."

Rita began to shake her head, but Gelson gave her a curious glance which stopped her. She looked at him startled, as if she had received a thought from him. *We'll stall,* he was telling her, *we'll make it look like we're doing it his way. Maybe something will happen. Play it cool!*

Gelson walked toward the console. "I suppose you want me to try to do something about that Army Air Force plane that's searching for us."

Zindel stared surprised. "Amazing! You read my mind perfectly. How you picked up the plane, I don't understand—but I grant your psychic powers are extraordinary, Gelson."

Zindel flipped a switch, and on the monitor screen they saw an Air Force plane hurtling through the sky. The screen tracked its flight overhead and it went out of sight. "Strange," Zindel murmured. "I would have thought—"

"Another one's coming," Guri said. "A helicopter. It's the search plane not in the range of your viewfinder yet."

Zindel looked at him. "Then, how do you know?"

Guri shrugged and tapped his forehead. "I can see it up here. Three-man crew. Pilot and two machine gunners. It has rockets and bombs."

Rita looked at Gelson, about to say something sharp, and suddenly changed her mind.

"Very interesting," Zindel said. "Now how would you propose getting rid of it?"

Guri frowned and rubbed the back of his head. "Well, there's two ways, offhand. I can either try to think a piece of metal on it to malfunction, like fall off or bend—or—"

"Never mind the second idea," Zindel said. "I like the first one. If you can do that, we have crossed a new frontier and will be on our way toward our goal."

Guri shrugged. "I thought the second idea was

worth hearing, anyway. I don't think it's been done before, either."

Zindel smiled. He relaxed in his chair and turned to face Gelson. "Very well. I owe you the courtesy of listening. After all, you apparently will become my strongest collaborator yet."

Gelson was leaning forward peering intently into the gray monitor. "It ought to be coming along soon. Darn it, I can hear the thing—"

"What was your thought, Gelson?" Zindel said, amused.

Guri turned his hands palms up. "I was thinking maybe I could send up a different kind of energy to disrupt the radar fix they have on you."

Zindel stared. "What gave you that notion? There's no way they could have done that."

"Maybe not before I came. But you have to remember, my body gives off a different kind of beat. Maybe that's what's bringing them in. They're tracking to me, Zindel, don't you get it? Come to think of it, maybe you really ought to forget the whole thing, and let me and Miss Quimby go free."

Zindel waved his hand. "Out of the question. But I can see now your second thought is more important at the moment for our survival. We can bring down the plane later. By all means, Gelson, let's see what you can do about interfering with the Army radar system. And incidentally, just how do you propose to do it?"

"I concentrate," Guri said. "I think hard about sending my energy current into space. If I can maintain it, the waves meet the radar waves and deflect them. At least, that's what I think will happen. But you're the scientist, maybe you know a better way."

Zindel shook his head. "Proceed with your

plan, please," he ordered.

Guri sat and closed his eyes. He appeared to be breathing very deeply. He brought his hands up slowly and extended them. "I feel something cooking now. Here goes."

The monitor picked up the Army helicopter. It came in from the southwest and hovered almost directly over the island. For a moment it swung there as if held by an invisible string. Then it climbed higher and veered to the west, toward Sausalito. It kept climbing, and then went out of view.

Zindel clapped his hands. "Excellent," he said. "But perhaps it was an accident. The pilot might have been heading that way."

Gelson opened his eyes. "What accident? I did it, I tell you. I was concentrating real hard. Sending up a very strong beep-beep."

Zindel bowed his head sardonically. "Wonderful. Then, you wouldn't mind a further demonstration, I'm sure."

"Like what?"

"Bring them back."

"Back over here?"

"Yes," Zindel said. "Then we'll know if you can actually do what you claim. That plane is out of sight now. If it returns, I'll have to go along with your claim."

Gelson shook his head and sniffed. "Jeez, make up your mind. You know, you can wear me out this way." He closed his eyes again, moved his lips, lifted his hands.

Zindel moved his chair closer, his hawklike face anxiously watching the screen. The set picked up a throbbing sound. It grew louder and stronger until the sound filled the room.

"There it comes," Rita said, pointing to a thin

127

cloud that suddenly appeared.

The helicopter came out from behind the cloud, and headed directly for the island. It veered left and right as if it was trying to decide where the centering force of the radar was.

"Bring it directly overhead," Zindel said.

Guri shrugged, his eyes still closed. His lips moved again silently and beads of perspiration formed on his brow.

The helicopter moved once more and hovered in the center of the screen, in plain view.

"Hold it right there, Gelson," Zindel commanded.

"Okay. Right there, as she is," Guri said.

"Now," Zindel said. "Let's see you do the first trick."

Gelson's eyes flew open and he stared. "Huh?"

Zindel snapped his fingers impatiently. "The metal part, remember? You said you could bring the plane down by thinking about some metal part. Making it malfunction, or whatever you do to it."

Gelson shook his head. "But maybe you don't understand, Dr. Zindel. If I do that, the plane will crash. Those men in it will be killed."

Zindel nodded succinctly. "Good boy! That's telling it like it is. Let's see you do it! Now!"

Gelson closed his eyes and muttered.

Joe Polo was lost in the labyrinth of Zindel's subterranean fortress. The corridors were long and seemingly endless, veering off at right angles into other desolate unmarked hallways. He appeared to be the only human walking about.

From Dr. Otto Compor's neurological ward, he had tried to stay within the inner core of the vast place, but without markings he was led far-

128

ther away. He knew Zindel would have some large central spot for himself and his prisoners, and he was sorry now he had so summarily put Dr. Otto Compor out of range of any more direct questions. That was an impulsive move he could regret, he knew.

He stopped, suddenly noticing something oddly different about the wall, tapped it and thought it sounded hollow. That suggested an elevator shaft, and Polo looked it over closely and found the recessed button. He pushed it and prepared himself for any sudden surprise. The door slid open and Polo poised on the balls of his feet, saw nobody in the car and stepped inside. The door closed.

There were no numbers on the panel board, no flashing indicator of where he might be heading. Polo shrugged his massive shoulders and resigned himself to the caprices of Fate.

The door slid open as the car stopped. A cold miasmic wave of air swept through the corridor. Polo walked steadily along the hall wondering if this was going to be the end of the line. He came to a conning tower and a large glass overlooking a huge staging area. He shook his head, amazed at Zindel's missile site.

Polo had the firepower on him to disrupt the operation, but put away the thought for the time being. The total effect would be to bring them all down on him, and that was no way to conduct a lifesaving operation. Polo wisely backed off and chose another corridor. He felt luckier almost immediately finding a small room. He walked past the open door swiftly the first time, and saw a lone clerk monitoring a TV board. Polo came back and walked in. The clerk looked up and apparently recognized the sentry's night jumpsuit

Polo had borrowed. He returned his eyes to the board and then looked up again suspiciously at his visitor.

Hitting him at the nape of his neck with a fast *shuto* karate chop, the man collapsed in a heap on the floor. Polo decided not to kill him and looked at the monitor screen. He saw an Air Force helicopter come into the picture, swing almost directly overhead, then veer and take off in a westerly direction.

In a few seconds, the ungainly bird came back, its huge props whirling and again it seemed to hover directly overhead. Polo peered intently at the glass, wondering how the Army had found Zindel's operation site so quickly, and then remembered talking of that possibility with Cantrell, with Gelson there.

Polo pictured Gelson now in some key room, the prisoner of Zindel, with Rita either on the rack or up for grabs with her life in the balance if Gelson didn't produce. Produce what? Polo thought, and then saw the helicopter again and knew.

He heard footsteps approaching and stepped back behind the door. The sound of the TV monitor gave up a funny grinding noise, but Polo couldn't take the chance of coming out to see what was happening. He heard the voices of two men as they came into the room. They stopped short and Polo knew they had spotted the man he had kayoed.

Polo stepped out confidently then, the long-bladed knife in his hand, stopping short at the weapons the two men carried. The larger one grinned, looking down his M3 automatic rifle at Polo's puny blade. The second one was short and stocky with wide shoulders and a barrel chest

130

and looked like a wrestler. He carried a sub-machine gun under one arm.

The larger one winked at his partner. "Looks like we got the guy who knocked out Ruby."

The other grinned widely and brought his gun up. "Yeah, ain't that too bad. Who you want to go first, Pete?"

Polo said, "My turn. Visitors go to bat first. It's a rule, fellas."

He threw the knife with surprising speed and the stocky man with the big gun stood there a moment with the blade in the center of his throat. He gurgled up a well of blood and while he was falling down knowing he was dead, Joe Polo went to one knee, grabbed the fallen weapon, and swung it against the bigger man's legs. He brought it up higher the next time jabbing sharply between the sentry's legs and the man opened his mouth to scream. Polo was on his feet then and swung hard and closed the man's mouth, smashing out his teeth, and breaking his jaw.

As he went down slowly like a stuck steer, Polo hit him at the back of his skull and the man lay still on the floor. Polo dragged both bodies across the room and slid them under a long table. He turned back to the TV monitoring screen and saw nothing now in the picture.

There were other dials on the board and Polo flipped them getting in turn views of the missile site, the psycho ward, the tunnel crew, the landing strip and finally, to his vast relief, he had centered in on Dr. Zindel with his prisoners.

Polo blessed his luck and reached for the sound tuner to bring their voices up. There was too much static to hear clearly and Polo wondered if Gelson was responsible. He looked for Rita and saw her at the edge of the picture. She looked unharmed and every inch as beautiful as she had been the last time Polo had been with her.

They were looking at the screen and their image was blank too. Polo tried to listen to what they were saying, but the sound disturbance was too much. He could pretty much guess what was going on after having seen the helicopter. Had Gelson brought it down? he wondered. Polo was certain Gelson could do almost anything with his strange psychic powers, and he knew that given that power himself, with the fate of a woman like Rita Quimby hanging in the balance, he would damn well cooperate with the boss, too.

Polo turned hearing a groan. It was the desk man he had chopped down when he first came in. Polo was on him in an instant, the knife retrieved and at the groggy man's throat. Polo twisted his head, and made him face the TV screen. "It's your life, pal. Where is that lab? Talk or die."

The man pleaded with his eyes and blubbered for mercy. Then, "Around the corner. First door to your right. Down steps. First left. Three doors. Go in center door."

Polo removed the blade and stuck it in his boot. "Let's hope I don't have to come back and kill you for lying."

He was out the door before the man could answer.

JOE POLO TURNED THE CORNER, as the man at the monitor had directed, suspecting a trap. He tensed going through the first door on his right but it led to another open corridor. He went down the short flight of steps, took a left, following directions. He found himself facing three doors, dead-end, at the top of the hall. Go in the center door, the man had said.

He pressed his ear close to the door and heard a low moaning sound. That wasn't what he had expected, but the thought of Rita being caught up and tortured nagged at him. He tried the door knob. It turned in his hand and he opened the door and went in cautiously.

The room was in utter darkness, no window or light relieving it, and the moaning sound was coming from deep in the recesses of its gloom. Polo stooped low, trying to accommodate his eyes to the blackness, addressing himself to the moaning sound. "Rita?" he said softly.

The moaning sound changed into an eerie wail. He took one more step forward and heard the click as the heavy door closed behind him. Polo didn't like that and found his way back to the door. He tried it and discovered he couldn't get it open.

Polo got out his pencil flashlight and played it over the lock mechanism. He saw no release lever and cursed briefly. The moaning sound came again and he put the flash in the direction of the opposite wall. His thin light picked up a figure huddled on the floor. As Polo drew closer, he saw it wasn't the girl. The face was strong and deeply tanned, the body hard and muscular. The eyes were staring and vacant. Polo dropped to his knees. "Mario, what the hell happened to you?"

There was no light of recognition in the eyes of the fisherman who had brought him out to the island, and given up his launch to the iron-jawed underwater monster of Dr. Zindel.

His jaws clenched and unclenched, his teeth gnashed at nothing, and his lips trembled and drooled. Polo touched the man's head. It was feverishly hot, covered with sweat, the sweat running down his face unchecked. Under the sharp light of the flash. Polo saw Mario's hands pinned at arms length to the wall.

"Did they hurt you, Mario?" Polo asked.

The man looked up at him unseeing, and then his eyes closed as his body cramped convulsively. Polo felt his stomach, the gut tight as a drum, then his wrist. His pulse was racing so fast, the beat couldn't be counted. It had to be a drug, Polo thought, something they had put into Mario when they got him out of the water. Perhaps they were getting him tired out and ready for Dr. Otto Compor's experiment room, putting him through the wringing-out paces as the preliminary to the operation procedure.

"Relax, pal," Polo said. "I got you into this mess. I'll get you out." He played the torch on the wall, and grimaced at the steel pinions and the chains at Mario's wrists. He pushed back the manacles and saw the red imprints of the needle, and then at the forearm vein, another mark of the hypodermic. There was no way he could guess what drug they had put into Mario, and no guarantee he could get him out alive, but Polo had his own code.

He stuck the barrel of his Colt .38 into the steel pin on the wall, strained hard with all his weight on it, and broke it free. He did the same to the one holding Mario's other arm and tried rubbing some circulation back through his wrists. He debated briefly about getting the manacles off the man's wrists, deciding to let them stay. They might prove to be a formidable weapon if Mario ever became conscious enough to help fight his way out.

There were three doors, Polo remembered. The man at the monitor had been smarter than Polo had anticipated. Take the center door, Polo mimicked silently. Hell! All three doors led into the same room. Talk about the lady or the tiger! But this was no time to reflect on how he'd been duped. He darted away to try the other two. They were all locked, he discovered, and he came back to the groaning figure of the fisherman, wondering what the next move was. As he hunkered over Mario's body, another wave of pain gripped the man, and his body heaved and rose in a tight arc six inches off the floor.

Polo saw it then, the thin markings of a trap door.

Trap doors could lead to pits with all kinds of horrible things in them. Polo knew, just as well as they could lead to a change of scene. He moved the heavy body of Mario to one side, and pried the long rectangular lid open.

The was a light below, perhaps twenty feet, and a steel-runged ladder. He went back to Mario. "Come on, pal. We're checking outta this dump." He tugged Mario closer to the opening, went through first and then brought the man's heavy limp body over his broad shoulders. Whoever had put Mario in here would sound the alarm once his disappearance was noticed, and he prayed for time.

Polo went down the steep ladder carefully, hand over hand, carrying the dead weight easily. Halfway down, he flashed his light around and saw another chamber very much like the dungeon the apelike man had carried him to. But there was no ravening leashed beast here, nothing but the heavy stones packed with moist earth, covered sparsely with straw, and a dripping water pipe.

Dumping Mario on the ground near the pipe, Polo played the cold water on his face. The man's eyes flicked open and there was almost a hint of life in them now. Polo nodded and heaved Mario on to his feet. The husky skipper's knees buckled and Polo caught him, steadied him, and held him close. "Come on, pal. Stick with me. We walk this one off. A drug is like booze. We walk it off. Let's go."

Zindel sat at his long winking console board adjusting his scopes. He showed Gelson and Rita Quimby the TV screens with the missile site and the tunnel gang crew. "You've already observed the neurological ward," he said drily, "so there's no need going over that aspect again. I'm sure you remember every detail, both of you, and are unwilling to furnish us a new subject for experimentation."

He flipped the screens off and turned to another, adjusting it so that Guri and Rita could see clearly. "This is San Francisco, as you probably know, the downtown area. The tape will now take you to the Golden Gate Bridge, and then we'll discuss your next attempt, Mr. Gelson."

The panorama unfolded and held on the long span of the beautiful bridge. Zindel turned to Gelson. "Well, do you think you can bring it down?"

Gelson's eyes boggled. "That big bridge? Hey, that's impossible. It would take something like an A-bomb to do that."

Zindel nodded. "True, the bomb could do it, and so could many bombs placed at strategic places. But we are interested now in seeing how much energy you can convey. As you may know, marching troops in ordinary one-step cadence can knock down a bridge merely by their vibrations. That's why they are given orders to break step when they march over any suspended structure. Your power is in vibrations, too, Gelson, at an intensity unknown to present-day science."

Gelson blinked. "Well, yeah, but I wouldn't know how to even go about it."

Zindel smiled tolerantly. "Approach it as you did the helicopter. That went down easily enough once you concentrated. Do you remember how you did that?" he asked.

Guri shrugged. "That one, I was trying to knock out some piece of metal. That was all. But I had to concentrate very hard because I didn't know exactly what piece of metal to focus on."

"Which part was it?"

"I figured finally the little pin that held the blades—and if that went wrong, the rotor mechanism couldn't work and it couldn't stay up in the air."

Zindel nodded. "Fine. That's pretty much what happened, I imagine. When my men get there and bring back the remains, we'll have the metal damage analyzed. But I'm confident it happened pretty much as you described it."

"I hope nobody got hurt," Gelson said. "How come your TV cameras didn't follow it all the way down?"

"Unimportant," Zindel said. "We're interested only in results. Now focus, please, on the bridge, and raise your vibrations. We can tell by clocking the magnetometer if your level is increasing."

Gelson looked puzzled. "What part of the bridge? How far away is it? Maybe I can't reach it with thought waves."

Rita broke in nervously. "Can't you pick something else for him to do, Dr. Zindel? There are a lot of people crossing that bridge in cars and—"

Zindel looked forbiddingly at her. "The advancement of science comes before human lives, Miss Quimby. Mr. Gelson is making history with these experiments."

"It won't be to his greater glory, nor yours, either," she said stubbornly. "Also I think you have your priorities mixed. Science is supposed to be the servant of us humans, not our master.

But then I suppose, like the other far-out megalo-maniac Dr. Ming, you're out to destroy us earthlings."

Gelson saw the darkened brow of Zindel and intervened quickly. "Well, you got a point there, Rita, but be reasonable. A bridge that size—what could I do to it? Even if I could knock a cable loose, they got hundreds of others all over it, holding the span up. Regardless of what Dr. Zindel thinks of my far-out power, I think I'm too far away to put a dent in the Golden Gate anyway. Maybe if I was on it, I might loosen a cable or two, but—"

Zindel interrupted smoothly. "I'm not interested in any theoretical discussion from either of you, if you don't mind. I'll give you ten seconds to concentrate on the bridge and do something to it, or I'm afraid Miss Quimby will have to be sacrificed."

Gelson blew his cheeks out and shrugged. "Okay, I'll try. But remember I ain't guaranteeing any results."

He closed his eyes and began to inhale and exhale, pumping his energy up. Then he looked at Rita as if to say, there's nothing at all gonna happen, why worry?—he leaned intently toward the fixed image of the Golden Gate Bridge on the TV monitor screen.

There was a knock on the door. Zindel raised his hand to Gelson. "Hold it, one moment, please!" As the knocking outside continued, he called out impatiently, "Yes, come in, Otto."

The door opened and a short man wearing a white coat stood there. He raised his hand deferentially toward Zindel.

"Dr. Kleeger? What is the meaning of this interruption?" Zindel snarled.

"I'm sorry, sir. There's been an accident. A terrible accident. May I come in."

Brusquely, Zindel waved him in and the mousy man walked across the room on sneakered feet with small mincing steps. "It's Dr. Compor," he said, when halfway there. "He's been—uh—torn to pieces."

Zindel stared. "What are you saying?"

The man gulped, nodding. "The ward—something happened—he was caught in there alone when suddenly the patients went amok. When we heard the noise, we broke in and had to beat them severely, drive them back with clubs and hoses. But it was too late, I'm afraid. They did some terrible things to Dr. Compor."

Zindel glared, baring sharp small white teeth. "What you are telling me is ridiculous, Kleeger! Where was my radioman at the monitor board? He was supposed to have been on duty."

The man sighed and twisted his hands nervously. "Well, there's been another accident there, too. He was assaulted by somebody—dressed like one of our own sentries, he said. Also two other guards were killed by this intruder."

Zindel's jaw dropped. "An intruder here? What are you saying?" As the man nodded again nervously, Zindel barked. "Send Felix to me, at once."

The man shook his head, paling. "I'm afraid that's not possible, either, sir!"

Zindel pounded the arm of his chair. "I gave you an order, Kleeger! Send somebody to get Felix and—"

"Felix is dead, too, Dr. Zindel. We found him in the lower east dungeon. I'm afraid the beast got to him."

Zindel stared coldly, his reptilian eyes glittering. "Was the beast let loose?"

"His tether was undone. But there was some other evidence there, too. An indication that perhaps the same person who killed the guards, did Felix in."

"What are you blathering about now, Kleeger?"

The little man in the white coat extended his hand. In it, plainly visible, was a long red-stained four-inch nail. "We dug this out of the base of his skull, sir."

Zindel wheeled his chair over quickly and took the nail from the palm of the other. He turned it over in his fingers and sniffed delicately. Then he wheeled to face Gelson. "Isn't this one of the objects Dr. Compor gave you to practice with?"

Gelson looked, and nodded. "Well, yeah, it looks about the same. I remember I bent the spoon and the key. I never did get to the ring or nail. But that blood—that wasn't on it."

Zindel frowned. "I'll take your word for it for now. Wait here, you and Miss Quimby. I've got to verify this for myself." He spun out of the room following the small doctor, and the door closed behind them.

Rita was remembering the agent she had met, and the idea that he might be behind some of these happenings was beginning to take hold of her. She raised her hand to tell Guri about this but quickly he frowned, shaking his head, silently pointing to the TV monitor.

"We're on the air, Rita," he said instead. "Maybe you want to sing something for the folks at home."

... 16

JOE POLO STOPPED COUNTING after he had walked
walked Mario around the small subterranean cell
five hundred times. He looked at Mario, breathing jerkily, his face red. "How we doing, pal?
Feeling better?"

Mario grimaced, throwing out his broad chest
and sucking air. "It's—it's coming. Maybe if I
had some fresh air—"

Polo grinned. "Be reasonable. When we break
out, you get all the fresh air you can eat. Right
now, you take what they got to offer."

An alarm sounded overhead, echoing loudly
through the open room above, sending overtones
throughout the walls. "Sounds like they found

something," Polo said. "I left a few bodies upstairs. They'll have us like rats in a box if they come down here. Can you move by yourself yet?"

Mario nodded, his throat hoarse. "I'll be okay —a little shakey." He looked down at the manacles over his wrists and the long chains swinging to the floor. "What the hell they do to me? All I remember is that thing picking me up outta the water. Like Jonah in the whale. Then I got hit on the head and—nothing!"

Polo nodded. "They slipped some kind of drug into you while you were out. Getting you ready for something. This is some kind of fun place."

Mario breathing hard, held up his hand for permission to catch his breath and rest. "Huh? What the hell is going on here? What sort of place is it? A nut house?"

Polo shook his head. "Not exactly. But there's a head nut here who thinks he's Hitler or Genghis Khan. He's put together a lot of scientific knowhow and is trying to parlay it into taking over the world."

"You're kidding."

"On the square, it's what's happening. Why do you think I'm here?"

Marlo shrugged and began to rub his wrists. "I dunno. Why the hell are you here?"

Joe Polo ticked them off on his fingers. "A kook named Zindel runs this operation. They got missile sites, bombs, rockets, troops, underwater monsters—who knows what else? And to make sure he can do more than the rest of the world, he just kidnapped a young guy—one of the best psychics ever—hoping to make him do his dirty work for him."

Mario blinked. "Like what?"

"His name is Guri Gelson. He can do fantastic

things with his mind. His thought waves can affect metal and radar waves. He's like a walking geiger counter, a kind of energy the world never knew about—on this planet anyway. I'm here to get him out—back to our own goverment."

Mario's dark eyes rolled. "Jesus—just you—against all this?"

Polo shrugged. "I got you to help."

"That's a lot."

"Zindel also kidnapped a young lady along with Gelson. We got to get her out, too. She works for the Army Air Force and probably knows a lot of confidential stuff Zindel would like to get out of her."

Mario pounded his fists together, rattling the long steel chains. "Okay—so I help you. Remember, we got no more boat outside to get away. What do we do—catch the ferry?"

Polo smiled. "Don't knock it—we may have to. But we got something more important to do before we get to that part of it."

"Like what?"

Polo gestured with his thumb to the sound above them of pounding running feet reverberating through the walls. "Like trying to stay alive, meanwhile. Come on, pal—we got to find a way outta this trap."

The stone walls looked solid but he tested each one with his hand hoping for a hollow sound that would indicate another chamber through a secret opening. He found it on the far wall, the sound a different kind of *thunk*. "Mario, c'mere. Maybe we can push this thing open."

"You get it started, kid," the skipper said tersely. "They look to be coming down here. Maybe I can hold them off."

Polo looked up, saw the guard's legs swinging

down from the open trap door above, on to the vertical steel ladder. His eyes gleamed. "Wait a minute. Why do we have to make it easy for them?"

He ran over and showed Mario what do. Each man put his shoulder to the ladder and tugged hard. The brace in the concrete wavered. Above, a man stood on the top rung and began to descend, closely followed by another.

"Now!" Polo said.

They heaved with redoubled strength and the ladder gave. They yanked it off its base and the two men yelled coming down.

"I'll handle it," Mario said. "You work on that opening."

Polo saw him waiting for the two sentries to get up, and then swing his manacled chains like a deadly flail. The men retreated, lifted their weapons. Mario's flail was faster and they screamed and fell back, as the heavy chains struck home. Mario lifted the chains back then, and reversed them. He swung them again in a vicious overhead double-arc. The sentries groaned and fell to the floor. Blood covered their skulls.

"Grab those guns and come over here," Polo ordered.

Mario scooped up the two automatic rifles and passed one to the special agent. Polo pointed to a line he dimly made out in the stone. Mario nodded and raised his rifle. Placing their shots in a vertical line, both guns blazing, something gave in the wall. Polo leaned on it and it swung open.

There was a heavy iron counterweight on the other side, and as they stepped through, the door closed behind them, plunging them into a stygian darkness. Polo flicked on his thin torch.

"Looks like a long tunnel," Mario said, peering ahead. "I see light."

Polo nodded. "Yeah, but I don't like this low stone arched roof. It's not high enough for us to walk through standing up straight. We'll have to go through at a crouch. Are you up to it?"

Mario grinned. "I'm getting better. Also, I smell water. Maybe this leads outside to the bay."

Polo hesitated. "That's no good. Outside is for later. We're in, we gotta stay in until we pull off the rescue. If we get out, we may not be able to break in again."

"Okay, you're the leader. I'm only going along with you so I can get paid back for losing my boat."

Before Polo could answer, they heard a strange sound, at first low, then rising higher. At first, in the gloom it was difficult to make out. Then, as Polo shot his torch ahead toward the approaching noise, Mario grabbed his arm. "It's water, pal. Looks like somebody is trying to flood us out. They opened a dike up ahead."

Joe Polo stared ahead. "Looks like we got two choices. We stay here and get drowned or try to race ahead and get out before the water floods us."

Mario thumbed at the stone door they had come through. "That water's coming through too fast. Why don't we go back through that door to where we were?"

Polo was at the door already looking for a purchase with his fingers. "We pushed it to get through. There's nothing on this side to get a grip on to pull it open again."

There was a deafening roar from the far end of the low aqueduct, and both men could see the water rushing in now in a swirling torrent. It

146

licked at their feet.

Mario shook his head. "There goes that choice, my friend. Nobody can go ahead with a million tons coming in. Looks like we gotta swim or drown."

"Hold it," Polo said. "I just remembered I brought along something, just in case."

Mario didn't argue as Polo urged him along toward the oncoming water. When they were far enough away to risk it, Polo pulled the pin on his grenade, started a slow, agonizing count, and then let it fly toward the stone door.

The explosion was deafening, and the concussive force knocked both men down. When they got up, the smoke was clearing. Polo pointed to a big gaping hole in the center.

Mario was shaking his head. "Man, you carry grenades in your pockets? What the hell do you do for a living?"

"Kill people," Polo said.

Water was clutching at their knees when they crawled through the shattered opening in the stone door.

17

ZINDEL'S DIABOLICAL CALM had deserted him. His pale face was distorted as he shrieked in rage. "Find him, you idiots!" He looked at the inert bodies on the floor, and having just witnessed the remains of his assistant Dr. Compor, Zindel was understandably upset. A lone intruder ruthlessly sacking his citadel was unthinkable. He raked the trembling guards with his yellow hot eyes.

"Flood the lower aqueduct, bar all escape routes. I want him brought to me alive, do you understand!" He bared his sharp white teeth. "I want to see the man who has dared to break in here and do what he has done. Then I'll think of a way to deal with him. But find him, or you are all in serious trouble."

A sudden thought struck him, and he wheeled away toward his private elevator. Why waste time pursuing a phantom down the endless corridors, when he had the one person in his room with the psychic power of clairvoyance and remote perception?

He entered the large control room where he had left Guri and the girl, a little surprised to find them chatting amiably opposite each other, relaxed as if awaiting the pleasure of his return.

Zindel wheeled his chair directly toward Gelson, stopping inches away. "We'll forget the bridge for the moment, Gelson. I've another need for your paranormal abilities. Let's see if you can guess what it is."

Gelson's voice was bland, his expression earnest. No instinct for self-survival, Zindel thought. The man is a servant to his psychic powers. He can't do anything but obey the phenomena of his transpersonal concepts.

Guri shrugged. "You're looking for the special agent, I guess. The tall dark man who came here —who came here—"

"Why did he come here?" Zindel snapped. "Tell me!"

Guri thought, shaking his head. He closed his eyes and when he opened them again, looked puzzled. "There are two thoughts, two pictures. I don't know which one is right."

"Fine," Zindel said. "Let's hear them both. I'll decide which one I like best. Continue, please."

"Well, in that case—the first thought is he came here to save me and Miss Quimby. And the second—" Gelson again hesitated.

"Talk!" Zindel commanded. "Don't analyze it.

Tell me." His eyes glued to Guri's face.

"—He came, he is going to—kill you," Gelson said.

Zindel's face darkened. "You can see that?"

Gelson rubbed his ear. "Well, yeah, but I told you, these pictures aren't always true. Sometimes they happen, and other times I miss, and it's like they go past in another zone."

"All right. We won't argue about it. Now tell me where the man is. You do remote viewing, I know. Can you see him?"

Guri closed his eyes again and began breathing slowly. His lips moved silently as if he were invoking personal forces in a prayer. Perspiration beaded his brow.

Rita, watching tensely, could stand it no longer. She sat bolt upright. "Don't tell him, Guri. Don't you understand? He's got to save us!"

Zindel's face darkened. He wheeled his chair over to hers and slapped her across the face. Her head recoiled and her eyes blazed angrily at him, but she said nothing, ignoring the red welts on her cheek.

"I warned you before," Zindel said, "to stay out of it. If he doesn't tell me now what he's seeing, I'm holding you responsible. By tomorrow morning, you'd wish you were dead—only you won't know who you are."

"I see water," Guri intoned hoarsely. "Water all over."

With a warning glance at the girl, Zindel spun back to Gelson. "You're only guessing, Gelson," he said sharply. "We are on an island in a bay. Naturally there is water all around us."

Guri shook his head. "No, this water is different. It is coming in here—like a flood—rising."

Zindel remembered suddenly his order to flood

the viaduct. "All right, there is water flooding in," he said casually. "Now where is the intruder?"

Gelson pointed toward the floor. "He is in the water—below us. I see the water reaching him—yes, beginning to flood over him. But he is doing something—there is another body there—the man is throwing something away—" His eyes closed and flicked open. He frowned. "Sorry, I lost the picture."

Zindel gnawed at his nails nervously. "You said before he was going to kill me. How is he going to do that?"

Gelson scratched his head. "I don't remember —the images come too fast. I see a lot of people screaming, but I don't hear any sound. But I think you are dead already. Something this tall dark man does."

Zindel remembered how Otto Compor had met his end, and comparing it to the precognitive thought now of Gelson, felt uneasy. He must remember not to be tricked into going near the psyche ward. He leaned forward, his eyes intent on Gelson's, searching for the tremor to tell him he was lying. "What is this man's name?"

Guri nodded. "Polo something. I can't see the first part."

Zindel straightened. "Joe Polo?"

Gelson smiled, lifting a finger. "That's it! You know him?"

Zindel scowled. "I've heard of him. An intelligence agent."

"Well, then," Guri said affably, "then you probably know how he works. I mean, in a business like yours, I imagine you get a lot of people like that, don't you? Trying to find out your secrets?"

151

"They don't live long enough to find out." Zindel said.

Gelson held his hand up. "I just got another flash. They're out of the water. Polo and the other man. The fisherman."

"Where?" Zindel rasped. "Where are they?"

The door opened quietly. A tall man with bulky shoulders stood there holding an automatic rifle. Another man stood in the open doorway behind him. "We're here," Polo said. He inclined his head. "Come in, Mario. I want you to meet the chief nut of this kookie factory."

He started walking toward Zindel. As he passed the center of the room, he saw Gelson sitting quietly, and near him, the girl. Polo smiled. "Everything okay?" he asked easily.

Rita nodded. Gelson stared, and said nothing. He watched Zindel moving away in his silent wheelchair. Polo shook his head.

"Save your energy, Zindel. You're dead no matter how fast your kiddie car will take you." He took a step forward, then faltered. His eyes looked surprised. He shook his head. "C'mon, Mario. Let's get this over with."

Mario came up alongside. He looked at Joe Polo, "Okay. What do we do?"

Polo waved his arm forward but again seemed unable to move. The thick muscles on his neck corded like ropes and he strained as if against an invisible force.

Rita screamed. "Stop it, Guri. He's the only one who can save us."

Gelson's face turned white, and his head snapped back as if he had been struck. He exhaled sharply, and suddenly Polo found he could move. He glanced at the girl and then at Guri. "What the hell was that?"

152

He was still shaking his head, Mario walking at his side, when Zindel's arm snaked out and touched his control board. There was a slight humming sound. Zindel whirled, a harsh laugh breaking through his masklike face. "I'm afraid you missed your chance, Mr. Polo," he said.

Polo stiffened held by the magnetic grid. Alongside him, Mario was trembling. The rifle fell out of his hands. A look of pain and bewilderment swept over the swarthy fisherman.

"What the—?"

Mario was falling stiffly to the floor. Polo held his position a moment longer, grinding his teeth angrily. He got his rifle halfway up when the current under his feet gripped him. He too began to shake like a leaf in a gale. Then, with a shudder, he fell stiffly, his feet rooted to the dangerous grid.

Zindel shook his head mockingly. "Wet feet only made it that much easier." He turned to Gelson. "I congratuate you. Your warning thought beam was nearly successful. It held him definitely, as securely as any force field. If it weren't for that foolish girl opening her mouth, I believe he would have killed me—as you predicted."

Rita paled, shaking her head contritely. Her hand went out to Gelson. "I'm sorry, Guri. I didn't understand. You were trying to keep them from stepping on it—"

Gelson shrugged. "It didn't matter. It was only a thought. Dr. Zindel could have stopped them anyway. He has steel knives imbedded in his chair, operating like torpedoes. If Joe Polo didn't step on the grid, he would have killed him and the other man quicker."

Zindel nodded. He patted the recessed slot under the arm of his chair. "I didn't think you noticed, Gelson," he commented caustically.

Guri shook his head. "I didn't. It was just—well, I kind of got the picture."

Zindel smiled wolfishly. "And what is the picture you get now, Gelson?"

Gelson frowned, shaking his head. "Frankly, it ain't good."

"I'm inclined to agree." Zindel pressed another button, and a swarm of guards came in through the door. He cut the current to the grid floor and waved his hand contemptuously. "I want those two under tight security, and made manageable by tomorrow morning when I see them."

As Polo and Mario were dragged away, the leader of the squad turned, gesturing toward Gelson and the girl. "What about those two?"

Zindel chuckled. "Take them in to Dr. Kleeger. I'll want special treatment for them, too. Tell him I'll be in his ward directly, and we'll discuss the treatment."

As the guard got Gelson and Rita to their feet, Zindel said mockingly, "Power is nothing, Gelson. Nothing at all. The real trick is in knowing how to use what you've got."

Guri nodded. "Yeah, I guess you're right. But it still won't do you any good, you know."

"What do you mean?" Zindel snarled.

Guri wagged his thumb toward the open doorway. "That fellow—Polo—he's still going to kill you."

Zindel pounded his chair, shrieking. "Take them away!"

18

POLO, STRIPPED TO THE waist, winced as he heard the blows from the adjoining cell and the groans of Mario. He strained against the ropes binding him, but he had been so brutally flogged that he had little strength left. His body was thick with blood and reddened welts, his face a gory mask. He licked his mashed lips with the tip of his tongue wondering how much more he could take from Zindel's punishment squad. They were big and strong, expert with their whips and their lead-gloved fists. He had no mirror handy to see what they had done to him, but his nose felt smashed from eye to eye, his cheekbone stung and throbbed as if it was fractured, and his breath caught on his ribs where they had kicked him with heavy boots.

Otherwise, Polo thought dully, looking down at his tied hands, he was in great shape. Ready to go another round with any three-year-old girl on the block.

His hair, matted with blood, was wet from the hosing they had given him to revive him the first time his body had given out. Then they had beaten and stomped him into unconsciousness again, and left him to deal with Mario next door. He heard Mario cry out again, and then there was silence.

He heard them leave the next cell, and then the clanging of the steel-barred door and the hollow-sounding click of their heels as they marched away down the long hallway.

"Mario," he called hoarsely. There was no reply. It had to be worse for the affable skipper from the Bay area after his drug-weakened state, and Joe Polo cursed under his breath, and his eyes roved the long high cell looking for some miraculous way out.

There was just the chair he was tied to, the bare walls, and the steel-barred door. No trap door on this floor, he noted, no window high on the wall. The only relief he saw was the duct near the ceiling, and he thought ruefully if he was a trained kangaroo maybe he could jump ten feet in the air and kick the vent in.

He shook his head to get the blood out of his eyes, and thought about Gelson and the girl. He had been unconscious when Zindel made his final threat, but Polo knew Gelson had tried to help him with the incredible force field that had prevented him from walking onto the grid, and Zindel would be getting even. Polo pictured that, possibly the psyche ward, and didn't like the thought. He thought of the smooth young body of Rita Quimby being subjected to a lot of Zindel's most fanciful thoughts, and he growled deep in his throat and in helpless rage, shook the chair he was bound to.

Polo became aware of a light humming sound. It seemed to filter down the long hallway, and then he heard it vibrating against the steel bars of his cell door. Polo's pulse began to quicken as he distinctly saw the bars begin to vibrate from this outside force. Jesus, he thought, what the hell is going on? A new death ray of Zindel's sent to seek him out? A new kind of laser beam that would turn the corridor and pick his cell-block out?

At the same moment, he felt Gelson touch him. He looked down, but of course Gelson was nowhere near. He heard Gelson's voice then, urgent and commanding.

Watch the cell door, Gelson was saying, *think about it with me. Let our minds join forces now as I send you the energy thought that will separate the bars. Pick one bar, any bar and concentrate on it. Now! Look at the bar. Think of the bar breaking! Will it to break! Now, now now!*

Polo shivered but listened and obeyed. Through his red-rimmed lacerated eyes, he sent his own violent thoughts toward the bar. He singled out the one nearest the big lock, centering all his remaining strength on it. Okay, come, break, you no-good fucking bar, Polo said silently. Break, break, break, you sonofabitch!

He sweated with the thought, his neck cording with the effort, brow sweating, and then his eyes goggled as he saw the steel shudder and seem to come apart before his eyes. He saw it snap, heard

157

the harsh sound, and then it flew across the room to land at his feet.

Polo didn't know how to thank Gelson, but assuming their minds were still attuned, he whispered silently, Thanks, pal. It worked. The mother came off and landed at my feet. Too bad you didn't do anything to that lock while you were at it—

He hadn't finished the thought when he saw the door shake more violently. Smoke came thinly from the center of the lock and then Polo heard it snap, as if a piece of metal inside had been broken.

Thanks, pal, you are the world's leading wizard, Polo said into space. Then he picked the iron bar up with his feet and got it into his hands and worked on the ropes until he had them off. He was breathing hard, sweating like a quarter-horse, but he recovered fast and got to his feet. He put his hand on the door, praying he wasn't wrong. There was too much riding on this one.

The door gave in his hand and Polo walked out.

The corridor was empty and he went silently to Mario's cell. He tested the steel bars, found them rigid as his had been and the door locked. Looking through the bars, he could see the blood-battered body of Mario on the floor. He was out cold, lying in a pool of his own blood, and Polo noticed they had done such a good job on Mario, they hadn't bothered tying him up.

He was wondering how he would get the door open when he heard the guard returning. Polo stepped back into the shadows.

The guard walked past and Polo chilled him with the iron bar at the back of his skull. He caught the man before he fell and dragged him to his cell. He got the cell keys, and threw the unconscious guard inside, draping him over the chair the way he had been.

Then he went back to Mario's cell, got the door open, went in and began gently slapping Mario awake. It took a long time but Polo was persistent, and he kept at it long enough, until finally Mario couldn't take any more and opened his eyes ready to fight.

"About time, baby," Polo said grinning. "I thought you wanted to sleep forever." He showed Mario the cell key. "Can you walk?"

"Like usual," Mario said, getting to his feet and falling on his face.

Polo helped him up, and they both groaned. "Okay, we do it a little at a time. If we can walk, we can kill people. You ready?"

Mario's puffed face hid his grin. But his voice was sure and unwavering. "Anybody you can kill, I can kill better."

"All right. Let's do it."

They staggered out of the cell. Then Polo remembered something. He leaned Mario against the wall, went to the next cell and frisked the guard. He came back smiling crookedly, showing Mario the nice long hunting knife with the long sharp blade.

"Now what?" Mario said.

"We go hunting," Polo said.

Gelson flopped down on the small cot exhausted and trembling. Rita sat watching him. They were alone in a private room of the psychosurgery ward. A guard stood outside the door patrolling the quiet corridor.

"Did it work?" Rita said.

Gelson brushed the hair back from his eyes.

"I don't know. I—I tried something. I felt we were making contact. I could see him clearly in his cell, tied to a chair. He was all bloody. They had beaten him severely. I think he got my message."

Rita wrung her hands nervously. "He would need more than a message. I don't trust that creepy Dr. Kleeger. What if he decides to operate on us before he sees Zindel? Have you thought about that?"

"That's possible but unlikely," Gelson said. "I'm getting my full powers back, and I don't think he'll be able to hold anything metal in his hands that might hurt us."

"Well," Rita said impatiently, "I don't think even a jerk doctor like Kleeger operates with a spoon or house key."

Guri smiled. "With a doctor like Kleeger, I might have to make him think he *has* to use a spoon for brain surgery."

She got up and began pacing the floor. The guard came back and resumed his position outside the door. Rita could see his legs through the lower mesh part of the door. "What about the teleporting stuff you're supposed to be able to do?" she said. "Can't you make us disappear from this room and into another?"

"That's not easy with people," Gelson said. "I did it once with myself—I think. But I was never sure, and didn't know how I did it, if I did. I'm mostly good on objects. Like I think I just teleported something good for your friend Polo."

"Like what?"

"I'm not sure. Something metal. I thought he could use it."

"He could use a gun," she said dispiritedly. "Did you send him a gun?"

Gelson shook his head. He closed his eyes and then opened them smiling. "Anyway, I think whatever I did, worked. He's not in the cell any more. I just tried to contact him but couldn't."

She looked dismayed. "Maybe Zindel had him taken out to be executed."

"No, I don't think so. I see the other man with him now. They're walking around looking for us or Zindel."

The guard outside clicked his heels sharply. They heard the soft whirring sound of Zindel's rubber-tired wheels. The door opened, and he sat there looking at them coldly, the guard behind him with raised weapon at the ready.

"I hope you're ready," Zindel said. "I'm sorry it had to end this way. Come along now."

Gelson raised his hand. "You're making a big mistake, Dr. Zindel. I'm getting my powers back now. Watch!"

He stretched out his arm. Zindel turned his head and saw the rifle float out of the guard's hands. It hovered in the air beyond his outstretched arms.

"Incredible!" Zindel murmured. "Now, can you make it disappear? Teleport it?"

"Easy," Gelson said. "Watch. Abacadabra, rifle —go away!"

Zindel stared. Rita watched open-mouthed. The rifle was gone. The guard looked at them stupefied. "I don't—"

Zindel waved him off and faced Gelson. "Maybe you and Miss Quimby will still live. Tell me where you sent the rifle."

Gelson shrugged. "It should be waiting in your control room. I'm putting it on top of your console now. There."

Zindel turned his chair around. "Come along.

If it's there as you say, there's hope for you both."

The guard stared uncomfortably as they moved off.

...19

DURING THE LONG WALK down the corridor, and
the ride in Zindel's elevator, Rita was speechless,
her mind shaken by what Gelson had done. If it
had actually happened, as it seemed to—and was
no trick, no illusion—then perhaps he had also
done what he had said earlier, managed to release Joe Polo from his cell. But, she told herself
cautiously, these things were impossible. A living
human being couldn't do things like that, going
against all the natural laws of physics. She could
accept his bending a spoon, imagining that perhaps the heat from his hands had somehow
curved the soft metal. The key bending was
a little more difficult to accept, although still in

163

the area of possibility.

But nobody, she told herself, nobody in this world, takes a heavy rifle out of a man's hands merely by looking at it, and giving it mental orders, saying the foolish magic word *abacadabra* and sportively telling the rifle to go away—as it had done!

As they headed for Zindel's control room, she steeled herself against disappointment, knowing this was their last chance to survive, if Guri had actually done the trick. Otherwise?

She hated to think of otherwise.

She glanced at Guri out of the corner of her eye. He seemed comfortable and relaxed, his head down as if in thought, his lips pursed. Was he still muttering the same magic incantation? Rita wondered. But she had made the unfortunate error of interrupting and breaking his concentration once, and she was not about to do it again.

Rita thought of the tall dark swashbuckling figure of the special agent, Joe Polo. It didn't seem at all possible that he could prevail against all the odds here in Zindel's fortress and come up a winner. The odds against it would be staggering. But she remembered the light in his eyes, the cocky determination, the easygoing way he had of dissembling his power. Well, maybe, she allowed herself to think, just perhaps maybe . . . and that would be another kind of miracle.

Gelson meanwhile was moodily silent, wrapped up in the configurations and conjectures of his own brain. He knew that he had done a great and marvelous thing in the mental service to Joe Polo. Unfortunately, he still didn't know for certain that it had worked. All he had was the feeling.

He knew he had to keep a tight rein on these fugitive thoughts, trying to tie them up to the problem and its end result so that he could repeat the performance. The thing with the guard's gun, well, now that was something else again, something really special. And Gelson was racking his brain now, trying to recall exactly how he had done such a remarkable thing.

Gelson had felt the power building up inside his body, almost like canned heat, like he had too much to eat and had to walk it off. That feeling of great tension and vibration inside his body, as if he had to use the current before it made him walk up walls. Jeez, he thought now, maybe I can do that!

Then there was the nagging thought, putting him down, that he had done nothing himself, but that *they*, the cosmic powers somewhere out there in space, had been alarmed over his condition and were trying to help him The more he thought of the recent resurgence of power, and the doubling of his ordinary effect, the more certain he was that They had been called in to bail him out. Perhaps directed by another Higher Being.

Perhaps it was the sign he had always hoped for, the indication of a little more personal attention, rewarding him for all the many years of bending the stupid spoons and warping the keys. As if somehow, the gods had taken pity on him for this little trick they had allowed him, and seeing that he had done it in fairly good faith, with an easy acceptance and grace, now they were prepared to take him a step farther.

His eyes rolled upward. What can I do? he asked silently. You know about this problem we got down here. Okay, so you know it will take a real big miracle to get us out of trouble. I don't want my head worked on by these jerks, and the same for Miss Quimby here, if you don't mind.

So what I'm asking is, are you people with me?

He hunched his shoulders, waiting for the thump of the celestial clap on the back, but there wasn't any. He rolled his eyes along the hallways and up to the ceilings and the high recessed lights. Nothing happened. There was no sudden bolt of lightning, no riven wall, no blazing bush in this desert.

Gelson sighed, letting the air out of his chest, his head dropping forward. It had to be all in his mind, he thought dejectedly. He was still a clown. He had somehow managed to get off a lucky trick and that was it. He didn't even know how he had done it.

Zindel opened the door and shouted. Gelson opened his eyes and saw the rifle there on the console. He rolled his eyes upward and again thanked Them silently. Anything you want from me, any time, he told them, it's yours. You don't have to make no appointments.

"Incredible, absolutely incredible!" Zindel was saying. His harsh bleak face was relieved now by a genuine touch of scientific fervor. Zindel knew all the laws of science, all the probabilities of physics, and he knew that what Gelson had done was impossible according to all natural laws. The man was a parapsychological genius! A genuine psychic superstar! This kind of paranormal experience was up with the greatest of extrasensory phenomena. And the experience shook Zindel now as he realized that science was not the only way to get at truth and universal solutions. The probability of the impossible, Zindel told himself. It was there in front of his eyes.

"I don't suppose you know how you did that,

Gelson," Zindel was saying.

Guri shook his head. "Well, like I'm not exactly sure. Dr. Zindel. I know I was thinking real hard—that the thing hadda go, know what I mean? And like I was putting some back spin on it—"

Zindel rolled his eyes. "Back spin?"

"Well, yeah—to get it to go back this way. I mean, that was easier than to turn it in the air, and then shove it off. So I just thought—go back, rifle—go back and get in there, in that big room he uses."

"That was all?"

"Well, let's see. Oh, yeah. I told it mentally where I wanted it to go. Up on the console here. That really was one of the best I ever did. But like I told you, I felt hot tonight."

"The door, Gelson. How did you make it go through the door?"

Gelson looked puzzled. "Oh, you mean because it was closed? Well, that's no problem. You just tell it where you want it to be. It figures it out itself."

Zindel's eyes glazed. "It? *It* figures it out? What are you saying, Gelson?"

Guri stared back. "Well, how else could it happen?"

"Obviously not the way you think it did," Zindel said caustically. "Things don't think. They can't figure out what they are supposed to do. It was your brain that guided it, told it what to do, and also how to do it."

Guri shrugged. "Okay, so how did I do it?"

Zindel rubbed his hands excitedly. "Somehow you broke up the molecules. Perhaps your kind of energy is like a proton beam, enabling it to disassemble objects in their molecular structure, separate them, pass them through a solid substance, and then reassemble them all again on the other side of the barrier." He mopped his forehead, and shook his head. "All quite impossible, according to scientific theory as we know it, but I'm a witness to what you've done. Tonight, my boy, you've made history."

"Gee, thanks, Dr. Zindel. Nice of you to say that."

"And I'm sorry I tried to coerce you into using your powers beyond your own wishes, Gelson. We'll have to be more careful about the things you do for us here."

"Oh, that's okay," Gelson said. "As a matter of fact, now that I did this trick with the gun, I'd like to try that bridge across the bay."

"You would?" Zindel said surprised.

Guri nodded. "Not to bring it down. But I mean, I'd like to see if I can unravel some of those steel cables at this distance. That way, nobody would get hurt, and you could get a better idea of how I work at a distance. Okay?"

Zindel rolled to the console and flipped the set on again. The Golden Gate Bridge hung there fixed in the center of his screen.

Gelson waved his hand at Zindel. "Better move back a little. I'm aiming that way and I don't want you to get hurt."

Zindel smiled and obligingly wheeled his chair a short distance away toward the center of the room. Rita held her breath wondering if Gelson really could do the impossible—reach the bridge from where they were, and do damage to it. It was all crazy, absolutely insane, and furthermore—

Zindel shouted, "Stop! You're burning up my set!"

Gelson ignored him, standing directly in front of the console, looking intently at the image of the bridge. Tendrils of smoke began curling from the console. The scopes began to swing and oscillate wildly, and a frantic chatter began in the magnetometer, rising in volume until it became a solid screeching tone.

"No, no," Zindel said, waving his arms. "Stop it! Stop!"

Gelson hooked his arms toward the image of the bridge, and hunched his shoulders. "Break, you goddam bridge, you pink fink, break a cable, break a leg, I tell you. This is Gelson, your master talking. You hear me, you cables out there? Break! Take off! Loosen a few wire strands for the West Coast. Come on, give!"

He's mad, Rita thought. Mad as a hatter. They're all mad here. I refuse to believe any of this.

She turned away from the set and saw a slight movement at the door. It opened and she saw Joe Polo come in, closely followed by the other swarthy, stocky man. Polo smiled and put his fingers to his lips.

He had taken two steps into the room before Zindel saw him. "Gelson, get away from that set," Zindel shouted and pressed the forward release of his chair.

Guri turned, saw Joe Polo and smiled. "Hi, guy," he said. "Remember now, don't step on that grid thing."

Zindel swore and his wheels spun, and then Gelson turned and faced him. "No," he said. "We don't want to do that any more. Wheel, do you hear me? This is Gelson speaking, wheel. Fall off."

There was a strangled cry from Zindel as his

169

chair tilted and one wheel slid off its axle. He was trying frantically to stretch out, to reach the console lever, when the other wheel fell off, and Zindel toppled to the floor. He glared at Gelson, and then as his eyes fixed on Polo, he smiled. His hand went out to the arm of his chair.

Rita screamed. "Look out! He's got those torpedo knives!"

"It's okay," Guri said. "I'll shut off the current."

Zindel watched open-mouth in horror as a thin plume of smoke curled at the arm of his steel chair. Then he heard the cracking noise, as the arm fell off, and then the clatter of knives as they struck the floor.

He sobbed in frustration, then lunged for the long-bladed knife. He had it in his hand, ready to throw, when Gelson said in that curiously flat singsong voice, "Sticks and stones can break my bones, but knives will never hurt me."

Zindel's arm wavered, and his eyes widened. The knife he held was slowly curling, its blade beginning a wide looping movement that ended with it doubling back over itself to meet and stop at the hilt.

"Hold it one second, Guri," Joe Polo said. As Gelson looked up, Polo whipped out the long-bladed hunting knife. His arm went back and his wrist whipped. The knife blurred and whirled in the air.

Zindel stared down at the blade in his chest. He started to say something but only a great gob of bloody spume came from his lips.

Joe Polo stepped over and looked down at the dying man. "I think we got a great rescue operation going here, Doc. It was either this way, or feed you to the psyche ward like I did Dr. Compor. This is better for a real talent like you, right?"

Zindel's eyes rolled upward. He nodded once. Then his head rolled to the side and he coughed and was dead.

Gelson was facing the image of the bridge again when Polo touched his arm. "Forget it, pal. We lost our boat and good as you are, you can't make us walk on water."

Gelson nodded. "No, but I can bend spoons, keys—knives. I even teleported that rifle in here from down below."

Polo smiled. "Well, not exactly. We gave you a little help there, pal."

"THE HELL YOU DID," Gelson said. "Nobody helped me—except Them out there." He indicated the outer cosmic powers deferentially with his open palm. "Rita here was a witness. You can ask her. I just gave the rifle a thought, gave it a little backspin, and told it mentally where I wanted it to go. Then—"

Polo laughed. "Then it fell down in the hall a little past the guard. Mario and I were over there, and we heard what you were saying. So we thought it would be a good idea if we kind of helped get that rifle in here on the console. It figured to have a great sobering effect on a scientific mind like Zindel. When they can't explain anything, they go soft and their brains leave them. Otherwise, he would have noticed."

"Noticed what?" Rita said.

Polo shrugged. "The guard had an automatic rifle. Good for 500 shots a minute. That was the kind of firepower Mario and I needed. So we substituted what we had, the Army carbine."

Gelson scowled and walked to the console and picked up the piece. "Hell, it's a carbine, all right, goddammit."

Polo patted his shoulder. "That's okay, pal. Everything else you did was terrific. But everybody knows that if there's one thing a human can't do, it's transport a solid object through another solid object."

Gelson nodded dejectedly. "I guess you're right." He replaced the carbine on top of the long console, and looked over across the room at the closed door. Then he shook his head and muttered something under his breath. "Abacadabra," he said. "I thought that was the magic word for real, that made it happen."

Polo smiled. "Well—" He broke off startled as he saw Rita's expression change. "What's wrong?"

She pointed to the console top. "Look!" she whispered.

Polo followed the direction of her startled eyes in time to see the heavy Army carbine rise off the top of the console. It rested at an angle in the air several feet above it and then levelled itself out and floated away toward the door.

They followed it trance-like with their eyes as it neared the closed door. They heard a soft sucking sound as it touched the heavy door.

Rita gasped. "It's gone!"

Polo gulped. "Through the door!"

Mario shook his head. *"Mama mia!"*

Gelson had his eyes closed and was still muttering under his breath. "Okay, now take a right and down the hall—"

Cantrell looked miffed. "I don't see why you have to kill everybody, Polo. There were a lot of questions we wanted to put to Dr. Zindel."

Joe Polo shrugged. "I didn't have much of a choice. But it's not a total loss. Gelson spent a lot of time with him. With the ESP talent he has, he can about tell you everything that Zindel had on his crooked mind."

Cantrell turned to Guri. "Is that a fact, Mr. Gelson?"

Guri blinked. "Is what a fact?"

Cantrell looked annoyed. "That you could read Zindel's mind. Tell us what plans he had."

Guri nodded. "Oh, yes. Sure, that was easy. He had a good scientific approach to the idea. Really had it all figured out."

"That's fine," Cantrell said. "Now would you mind telling me so I could relay the information to Mr. Adams over at State?"

Gelson shook his head. "Oh, no, I couldn't ever do that."

"Why the hell not?" Cantrell snapped.

"Because I can read your mind, too," Guri said smiling. "You want to know for the same reasons Zindel did."

"What reason is that?" Cantrell barked angrily.

"Power," Guri said. "You want power. That's what you and Adams were going to use me for. Your own power."

Cantrell glared at Joe Polo. "What the hell have you done with him? I thought he was going to work for us," he said in confusion.

"He's been under a lot of pressure," Polo said. "It's made Gelson a lot smarter."

Cantrell looked around. "I still don't understand how he did it. Somehow he was able to disrupt our radar pattern and keep our observation plane away until you had things under control."

Joe Polo tapped his head. "It's a trick, Cantrell. He's got a magic word that he sends out in thought waves. Somehow it works for him."

Cantrell's lip curled. "Magic word! That's a laugh."

Polo nudged Gelson. "You got nothing to lose now, Guri. The Army's taken over the whole place, and Zindel is dead. Show the man what you can really do if you want to."

Guri stood smiling, shaking his head shyly. "Well, I dunno—it would make a terrible mess."

"What would?" Cantrell said.

Gelson nodded toward the image on the console screen. It still held the Golden Gate Bridge squarely in its center. "Like bringing that down. You know, with vibrations."

Cantrell snickered. "The Golden Gate Bridge? You're going to knock it down? This I gotta see. What do you say, Allagazam? Something like that?"

Gelson shook his head. "No. I say abacadabra."

Rita pointed. Her mouth opened and nothing came out. Her eyes goggled. Finally, she gasped. "Look!"

Cantrell, startled, turned his head in time to see the TV monitor screen shake violently. Then slowly the big Golden Gate Bridge seemed to buckle in the center. Smoke swirled along its span as cables snapped and girders slowly toppled. He could see the cars along the bridge catapulted into the air, spin in space and then fall. The bridge buckled inward, flexed upward for an instant, and then to Cantrell's horror, it snapped in the center.

Then as they all watched, the bridge fell out of the center of Zindel's TV monitor screen. The screen remained blank with nothing in the picture.

Cantrell rushed to the phone. "I don't believe this." He barked a number and spoke rapidly. He listened, said, "What?" Then, he slowly put the phone back on its cradle and stared, his ruddy face ashen. He pointed a shaking finger at Gelson. "Do you realize what the hell you just did, you crazy bastard?"

Gelson nodded. "No one's hurt, I can promise you that," Guri said, a lopsided grin on his face. "Besides, you gotta admit, it beats bending spoons."

THE END